DANCER
IN THE WINGS

Books in the series

DANCING PEEL
DANCER'S LUCK
THE LITTLE DANCER
DANCER IN THE WINGS

DANCER
IN THE WINGS

by

LORNA HILL

Illustrated by Anne Grahame Johnstone

AWARD PUBLICATIONS LIMITED

ISBN 0-86163-841-7

Text copyright Lorna Hill 1958
Illustrations copyright © Award Publications Limited 1997

First published 1958 by Thomas Nelson and Sons Ltd
This edition first published 1997
Second impression 2003

Published by Award Publications Limited,
27 Longford Street, London NW1 3DZ

Printed in Singapore

CONTENTS

1	Farewell to a House	7
2	Rehearsal	18
3	On Tour	31
4	Oh, for a White Ship!	41
5	The *Flora MacDonald*	51
6	At Sea	66
7	The Isle of Arran	75
8	The Mischief Maker	82
9	In Tobermory Bay	91
10	Loch Coruisk	104
11	Lost – One Dancer!	113
12	The Isle of Skye	134
13	The *Flora MacDonald* Again	143
14	The Exciting News	148
15	Annette Returns to London	157
16	The Stranger	163
17	The Celebration	170

1 FAREWELL TO A HOUSE

The family had lived in the condemned house in one of the small back streets near Covent Garden for some years. The house had been repaired, of course, but things had gone from bad to worse. A large jagged crack had appeared down one wall and the front doorstep had sunk.

'Damage to the foundations,' said the sanitary inspector gloomily when he called to see what could be done about the water that trickled down the kitchen wall from October until April. 'Time it was put on the List.' He meant the list of houses ready for demolition. 'See you in a brand-new council house by the spring.'

But the spring hadn't seen the Garretts in their new home, nor had the summer, and now it was the middle of February, and they were only just moving out.

When the last echo of the closing door had died away there was a slight sound in the kitchen, and from a dark hole at the side of the boiler came a lean tabby cat. Someone had given her to Jimmy on his fifth birthday, and for a short time, while she remained a kitten amusing them and making them laugh at her absurd gambols, she had been the family pet. But when she grew into a striped, anxious-looking tabby with a long thin tail they ceased to find her amusing and no longer wanted her. They weren't actively unkind to her – they just forgot about her. Most of her food she got out of the dustbins of the houses near by, but she always returned to the Garretts' house, which she still regarded as her home. She had crept in beside the boiler the night before, while there was still some warmth, had made a comfortable bed for herself on two old sacks, and there she had had her family, a motley assortment of five kittens – two black, two black-and-white, and one striped like herself. She stretched herself and yawned, then looked round for some food. Finding none, she went back to mothering her kittens, licking them all over and purring loudly.

At intervals throughout the day the cat jumped down into the deserted room and searched for food. She managed to insert her paw into the larder door and pull it open, but there was no food there either. She jumped up on to the draining-board, and seeing a little pool of milk lying in the cracked sink, drank it up thirstily. A ray of the setting sun streamed through the narrow window between the chimney-pots of the house opposite. The cat sat in its warmth for a few minutes, then hurried back to her babies.

The days passed, and the house grew colder and colder. Snow was falling outside, and the sky, seen through the window (now covered with a film of dirt) was a yellowish grey. The cat grew hungrier and hungrier, and the kittens began to mew piteously with cold and starvation. Try as she might, the mother cat could not keep them warm with her thin body. She began to lose her milk and one of the kittens, the weakest of the five, died during the night. The other four grew gradually weaker and less vociferous, and soon another of them died. The mother cat knew by instinct that unless she found food quickly, her whole family would perish. She scratched at the outside door in a vain attempt to open it.

Outside a gale had sprung up. It rocked the house to its foundations, rattling the windows and sending a spatter of hail against the panes. And then suddenly an extra strong gust of wind forced its way through the cracked windowpane, and, with a tinkle, the glass fell to the floor, leaving a star-shaped hole through which the snowflakes eddied.

The cat heard the sound of the glass and felt the cold inrush of air. She gathered herself together and leaped towards the broken pane. A week ago she could have reached it easily, but now, having eaten nothing for so long, she had little strength left. Again and again she leaped, only to fall short. And then, with a last despairing leap, she was through, and had landed on the pavement outside the house. One of her paws had caught the jagged edge of the glass and was badly cut, but apart from that she was uninjured. Leaving a trail of blood behind her, she limped towards the nearest backyard where she knew there was an uncovered dustbin. Rummaging in it, she found some crusts of bread and a scraping of stale fish. Then, although she was still very hungry, she limped back to her kittens, leaping through the hole as before, and cutting her other paw in the process.

Who can fathom the mind of a cat? The thin tabby attributed the death of her babies to some evil influence in the house and she determined to leave it before any more of her children were snatched from her. She picked up one of the remaining kittens, whose eyes were just beginning to open and look round at the inhospitable world into which it had been born, and carried it to the window. Her strength had come back a little now, owing to the food she had eaten, and she managed to leap through the hole with the kitten in her mouth. She carried it away between the rows of houses and out into the main street, where she crept along as close as possible to the wall. The hurrying people were all far too intent upon getting home as quickly as possible to notice her – all, that is, except one girl who was standing at the bus stop on the opposite side of the road. The girl's face was pale with cold and fatigue for she had had an especially tiring day. She was a ballet-dancer, and she lived in a convent home in the West End of London, just off Oxford Circus. She had risen

that morning at half-past six and gone to Mass in order to please the Mother Superior, then dashed back to breakfast, which was eaten in silence, and perhaps this was just as well, thought Annette, since most people were in a hurry in the mornings. At eight-thirty she had crammed on her coat, snatched up ballet-shoes and shoulder bag, and set off for her class.

Fortunately the Cosmopolitan Theatre, where the class was held, wasn't far away, but there were seven

11

flights of stone stairs to climb when you got there. After the class, which all dancers, no matter how exalted, submit to daily, came a rehearsal of a new ballet, then time off to snatch a sandwich and a cup of coffee. More rehearsing, a costume fitting, and by this time it was four o'clock. Although Annette longed for a cup of tea, she set off for Covent Garden, where, in one of the little back streets under the shadow of the great Opera House, she knew she would find a particular make of ballet-shoe. She was supplied with a certain number of shoes by the company, of course, but they didn't suit her feet as well as those made by the little Italian in Thames Street. At the moment she was only a member of the corps de ballet, and had to wear any old shoes; but one day, thought Annette, she would be in a position to demand shoes made specially for her by the Italian shoemaker, Umberto Corregio. For the present, she would buy her own.

So this was how Annette Dancy happened to be waiting at the bus stop at Covent Garden. It was now six o'clock and quite dark, but by the light of the streetlights the girl watched the cat, fascinated. It was such a thin, hungry, anxious-looking cat for one thing, and then it was obviously moving house and taking its family with it. Annette loved all animals, and she didn't care the least bit whether they were aristocratic or not. She thought a cat with kittens, even a nondescript tabby, the most lovable thing you could wish to see. She watched the cat carry first one kitten and then another across the busy road and into an alleyway on the opposite side and disappear into the backyard of a house near by.

I do believe she's hurt, the girl thought, as her bus came and went, and she only noticed when it was halfway down the road. She's limping, the poor little thing!

Back in a moment came the cat, crossed the road, dodging between buses and cars, and reached the far side in safety. She had evidently deposited her two kittens in their new home and was going back for a third.

I wonder how many she's got? thought Annette curiously, and while she was wondering the cat appeared once more carrying a third kitten. For a moment Annette's attention was diverted – a bus had appeared far off and she was trying to see if it was hers. She mustn't miss another one or she'd be late for the evening rehearsal. Annette, it may be said, was never late for anything concerning her dancing – not even a class. Although, being only sixteen, she was the youngest member of the company, she was certainly one of the most conscientious.

Oh, no – it wasn't her bus. She wriggled her feet, which were like blocks of ice, and looked round for the cat, and it was at this moment that the tragedy happened. A car shot round the corner. The cat tried to jump clear, but in its enfeebled state and encumbered by the kitten in its mouth it was unable to reach the kerb. The car ran over it, killing it instantly. The kitten was flung clear and landed at Annette's feet, mewing feebly.

'Oh, you poor darling! You poor darling!' she cried, picking it up. She ran over to the cat which, after one spasmodic jerk, lay motionless in the gutter. 'She was carrying her baby and you killed her, you horrible man!' She stared after the car through her tears. 'You horrible man.'

Several people in the bus queue echoed her words, and some of them fondled the kitten, but none of them offered to take it from her. They one and all averted their eyes in disgust from the body of the poor mother cat lying in the gutter.

I wonder what I ought to do with it? thought Annette, looking down at the half-blind morsel of fur that nuzzled her hand in a vain attempt to find warmth and food. Then she remembered the other kittens she had seen the cat carrying. There had been three of them altogether. Where were the other two, and were there any more? She walked down the road and found the alleyway leading into the yard of a house. The faint sound of mewing came from a nearby shed. Yes, there were the kittens – two of them – inside an empty barrel. There was a light in one of the windows of the house so Annette knocked on the door. After a few minutes a woman appeared with her hair in curlers.

'Please . . .' faltered Annette. 'Have you got a cat – a striped tabby, because if it's yours, it's just been run over.'

'Cat?' echoed the woman. 'We ain't got no cats 'ere. It'll be from one o' them empty 'ouses.'

'Then you don't want the kittens?' said Annette. 'There are two of them, besides this one.' She disclosed the tiny creature in her hands. 'They're in your shed.'

'In my shed indeed! I like that!' exclaimed the woman. 'Wait till I find them! I'll sort them! Drown them straight away – all the lot. That's what I'll do with them.'

Oh, no you won't, thought Annette. She dashed into the shed and, picking up the two mewing kittens, dropped them into the pocket of her coat. Then

she gently dropped the third one in beside them. Having done so, she left the yard, and went back to her bus stop. There was still no sign of her bus – most likely it had come and gone while she was talking to the woman.

As she stood there, the words the woman had said came back to her mind: 'Empty houses . . .' Yes, the cat had certainly come from that direction. The question was – were there any more kittens still left in the house? She couldn't go away without making sure. She pulled a torch out of her shoulder bag and hurried across the road.

It was anything but a nice feeling poking about among the dark, empty houses – even with a torch. All sorts of frightening stories came into Annette's head. She'd always been told by the nuns at the convent home never to go near empty houses after dark. In fact it was best to keep away from them altogether, they said. Undesirable people of all kinds haunted places like this, and no one was safe. Annette, flashing her torch in the dark corners of the tumbledown buildings, could well believe it. She felt like a character in one of Dickens' novels as she poked about. And then she saw the trail of blood left by the cat, and the window with the jagged hole in the pane.

'I do believe she must have jumped out through it with the kitten in her mouth!' she exclaimed.

She pushed open the door and went inside, not without some trepidation. There was a mouldy smell of general dampness. The cold sank into her very bones. It was almost impossible to believe that any-one had ever lived in such a place. She flashed her torch round the empty kitchen and picked out a small object lying on the floor. It was a dead kitten. A trail of blood led Annette to the old boiler, and then she saw the two old sacks and the second dead kitten.

For some strange reason, Annette couldn't bear to leave the dead kitten lying on the floor. She picked it up and put it on one of the sacks with its fellow. Then she went back to the bus stop and picked up the dead mother cat, who was by this time lightly covered with snowflakes. She carried her into the condemned house and laid her tenderly beside her two dead kittens, and covered them over with the second sack. With the tears running down her nose she left the house, gently shutting the door behind her.

2 REHEARSAL

All the way back to Oxford Circus, Annette pondered over the problem of the three kittens. She knew they were far too young to lap milk, so how was she to feed them? Then she remembered how Angus MacCrimmon, the vicar's son at home, had fed a tiny kitten with a doll's feeding-bottle, so she slipped off the bus at Piccadilly Circus and found a little shop that sold children's toys. Here she bought three doll's feeding-bottles, much to the amusement of the man behind the counter to whom she told the whole story of the tragedy. And now for milk to put in the bottles. Fortunately there was a chemist's next door to the toyshop, so she bought a tin of dried milk, intended, of course, for babies.

It wasn't worth waiting for another bus, so she took several short cuts and arrived at Oxford Circus in a very short time. She had made up her mind – the kittens must go to the rehearsal. She realised that unless they were warmed and fed immediately they would die. In fact, feeling carefully in her pocket, she wasn't sure if they were still alive now. But yes, she could feel them moving, though feebly. Oh, well, it wasn't as if she was anyone important. She wasn't even understudying the principal dancer. She'd probably never be missed out of the back row of the corps de ballet, and anyway she'd be there for the last part of the rehearsal.

When Annette reached the dressing-room it was empty, as might be expected, since the rehearsal had begun long ago. She hung her coat on a hook with the kittens still in the pocket. They were safe there, she thought, for the time being anyway. Near the fireplace stood an electric heater of the convector type with holes in the top. You couldn't boil anything on it of course, but she thought it might warm the milk. Accordingly she shook a little of the powder into a mug and mixed it with cold water, then added some warm from the hot tap. After which she filled the three little bottles, and stood two of them on top of the convector while she tackled the first kitten. It was wonderful to see how

the tiny creatures took to this novel way of feeding – or perhaps it wasn't so wonderful, considering that they had had nothing to eat for a very long time and were, in fact, on the verge of starvation. Very soon Annette had three contented kittens, warm and full of milk, peacefully asleep on her lap. She found a small box that someone had discarded, warmed her beret and put it inside. Then she put the box with kittens in it on top of the convector, and covered them up with her scarf.

'I do hope they don't get *too* hot,' she said a little anxiously as she undressed and put on tights and jumper ready for the rehearsal – or as much of it as remained. 'I also hope Monsieur Georges is in a good temper!'

But Annette's luck was out. Her much-loved Monsieur Georges was not in the roof studio, where the rehearsal was being held. Long before she reached the top of the last flight of steps she could hear Miss Marty's rasping voice giving orders. What could have happened? Miss Marty took classes in the school, but very rarely rehearsals. Annette had an idea that Monsieur Georges didn't really like Miss Marty, although he realised at the same time her good qualities as a teacher. Marion Marty had held all sorts of important positions before she had come to the Cosmopolitan School of Ballet, and indeed the school was lucky to get her. So said the authorities, and of course Monsieur Georges had nothing really against her, except a vague antagonism. Annette didn't like

Marion Marty either, and neither did the ballet-mistress like Annette. For one thing, Annette was Monsieur Georges's favourite, and for another she hadn't enough brilliance in her dancing to suit Miss Marty. Miss Marty liked brilliant dancers. To her, a brilliant technique was everything. She put virtuosity first, whereas Monsieur Georges put it – well, perhaps not last, but some considerable way down in a young dancer's attributes. Marion Marty liked the brains to be in the feet of the dancer; Monsieur Georges in his or her head.

'And where, Annette, have you been, if I may ask?' demanded Miss Marty when Annette tried to slip in with the other members of the corps de ballet, in the vain hope that she hadn't been missed. 'Had you forgotten about the rehearsal tonight? Or perhaps you had more important things to do?'

'I'm very sorry, Miss Marty,' said Annette. 'I missed my bus.' She didn't mention the cat or the kittens. Monsieur Georges would have understood about them, but not Miss Marty. In fact it was well known that she hated animals – and especially cats.

'Your bus?' cried the ballet-mistress sarcastically. 'I think you must have missed a whole fleet of buses! Do you know what time it is? It's now half-past eight.'

'I'm sorry,' said Annette again.

Miss Marty didn't answer. She tossed her shoulders, as if to indicate that Annette was past praying for, and the rehearsal proceeded. Annette danced badly, which was scarcely to be wondered at when you consider all her exertions. Not that anybody noticed except herself; Annette was always her own sternest critic. Miss Marty pointedly ignored her, and the rest of the company saw nothing wrong. Nearly everyone slacked at rehearsals anyway. But to Annette things were very wrong indeed. She always did her very best at all times and danced as well at rehearsals as before crowded houses. Tonight, however, by the time the rehearsal ended, round about nine o'clock, she felt as if she were dancing in her sleep. Having eaten nothing since lunch-time, she was light-headed from lack of food and her feet and head ached unbearably.

'Och, now, you look about all in,' said Irish Paddy Dolan, Annette's best friend. 'Tell me, now, what was it you were doing tonight, for it's me that's knowing there's more to it than just missing your bus!'

At that moment there was a squeal from the direction of the dressing-room. The kittens in their box on top of the convector heater *had* got too hot, and were letting the world know it in no uncertain fashion. You could hardly believe three such tiny kittens could make such a loud noise!

Annette pushed aside the squealing girls and rushed to her foundlings.

'Miss Marty! Miss Marty! Annette Dancy has got a whole lot of kittens in the dressing-room,' cried a girl called Simonetta, who was one of Annette's sworn enemies – Annette having (so Simonetta thought) stolen her part in the film the company had made.

Miss Marty came rushing from the staff dressing-room next door.

'Kittens! How dare you bring these animals here, Annette? Don't you know it is forbidden to bring animals into the theatre or the dressing-rooms?'

'It's only for a moment, Miss Marty,' said poor Annette. 'I'll take them away the very second I'm dressed.'

'But why did you bring them here in the first place?' demanded the ballet-mistress. 'Where do they belong? They must belong to someone. You must take them back there at once – at once, do you hear?'

And then of course Annette had to tell the whole story about the cat and the condemned house.

'What could I do with the poor little things?' she said when she had finished. 'I couldn't just leave them to die.'

'They will have to die in any case,' said Miss Marty coldly. 'One cannot keep three stray kittens. They will have to be drowned. I will see to it.'

'They will *not* be drowned!' cried Annette, standing over the helpless kittens like, as her friends said afterwards, a tigress defending her young! 'After all they have gone through, and after I've got them nice and warm and full of milk – to be drowned! No, it shan't happen!'

'You dare to disobey me!' exclaimed Miss Marty. 'Very well, but I shall not forget. You may be sure of that.'

'I'm sure you won't!' cried Annette, goaded. 'But Monsieur Georges will understand when I tell him. He's not like you, Miss Marty, he – ouch! What are you standing on my foot for, Paddy?'

'Shut up, Annette!' murmured Paddy in such an urgent whisper that Annette, startled, said no more.

The irate Marion Marty gave her a last scathing look and swept out of the room.

'Annette, mavourneen, why, *why* did you have to say that to her at all? Why did you have to do it? It's meself that was trying to stop you, and giving you all the warning looks I could, and standing on your feet, and you not paying me the least bit of attention whatever!'

'What's the matter?' asked Annette. 'Has something happened? You look so strange, Paddy! Tell me what it is.'

'You'll look even stranger than Paddy when you hear,' put in Simonetta triumphantly. 'Mighty strange you'll look.'

'It's Monsieur Georges,' said Tania, another of Annette's friends. 'He should have taken the rehearsal tonight.'

'Yes, I know. Why didn't he?'

'He came along all right,' said Tania, 'but he was ill. We could all see how dreadfully ill he was, but he insisted on taking over from Marion, who'd been carrying on until he arrived. And then – and then – '

'Go on,' said Annette, a sick feeling coming over her.

'And then he collapsed, the darlint,' said Paddy, taking on the story. 'Oh, it was awful! He seemed to have lost the power of his legs. One of us rang up the hospital, and they sent a doctor, and he took one look at Monsieur Georges and then sent for the ambulance, and they took him to hospital.'

'He asked for you especially, Annette,' said Tania. 'He said in a sort of whisper, "Where ees my leetle one? Tell her – tell her . . ." but he never got out what we had to tell you.'

'Oh, how awful! How awful!' cried Annette. 'And I wasn't there!' She never thought of blaming the cat or the kittens as some girls would have done. She didn't even wish she hadn't done what she had. She'd *had* to do it. Monsieur Georges would have wished her to do it, she knew he would. The tears ran down her face as she gathered up the three kittens and put them, still in the beret, into her pocket.

'I couldn't leave them to die,' she kept repeating. 'Monsieur Georges wouldn't have wished me to do that.'

'It's sure I am that he wouldn't,' agreed Paddy. 'All the same, I am wishful that it hadn't happened to you, Annette, mavourneen. Our Miss Marty will have her knife into you all right, and it's she who is to take over while he's ill, so they say.'

'Oh, I can't believe it, I can't!' cried Annette.

'Well, who else is there?' put in Tania. 'There simply isn't anyone.'

'No – I suppose there isn't,' Annette had to agree.

'And now perhaps the people who are *really* good will get a chance,' said Simonetta nastily.

The next day the ballet company knew the worst – that its beloved ballet-master, Georges Reinholt Dutoit, had suffered a severe heart attack.

'It's too terrible even to think about,' said Paddy. 'Why, only the day before yesterday he was showing us how to do entrechats *six*, and now –'

'And now they say he may never walk again – let alone dance,' said Tania.

'I'll bet he will though,' exclaimed Annette. 'They don't know Monsieur Georges as we do! If he makes up his mind to walk, he'll walk – doctors or no doctors!'

But when she had seen him in hospital she didn't feel so sure about it. Hospitals, especially the big ones, are cold, impersonal places at the best of times, and Monsieur Georges, such a dynamic personality in his own little world of the ballet, was now little more than a number in the ward where he lay.

Annette found him lying there, eyes closed, linked to an assortment of machines and monitors, and she

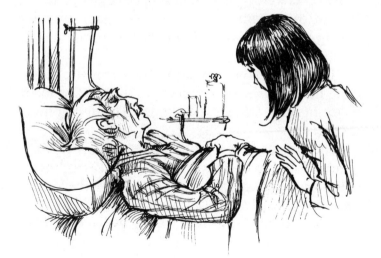

couldn't even speak to him. After a few moments she turned and ran headlong down the corridor.

At last Annette found herself near a door which bore a large notice: AMBULANCES. Her imagination ran riot. In her mind's eye she saw people being carried in, dead or dying, on stretchers – one every few minutes! Unfortunately she never found the door by which so many of them came out – cured!

Having escaped from the hospital she walked on aimlessly, and came at length to the Embankment, where she sat on a seat and watched the murky water flowing past.

At teatime she pulled herself together, went slowly back to the convent home and climbed the many flights of stairs to her room. The kittens, warm and cosy in her workbasket which she had made into a bed for them, greeted her eagerly and vociferously. Their eyes were by now almost open, and they looked round them with an innocent blue gaze, nuzzling each other and making funny little panting, hissing noises.

'I do believe you're swearing!' said Annette, forgetting her sorrows for a moment as she fondled them. 'You mustn't do that, you know. This is a convent home!'

There was a knock on her door, and Sister Marie Theresa appeared. By now all the sisters, as well as the Mother Superior, had heard the story of the kittens, and one and all approved of Annette's action. That was one thing about nuns, thought Annette. They might be stuffy; they might spend an awful lot of time praying, but they were kind. No talk about drowning the kittens from the sisters of the convent home. They would keep one of them in the house here. Although they already had two cats, one more wouldn't make any difference. And then the Mother Convent could take another. Yes, and a home should be found for the third one, never fear. When people heard about the tragedy they would come forward and offer. And they did too! Homes could have been found for a dozen kittens! But of course all this is in the future. At the moment, Sister Marie Theresa's white-swathed head and shapeless black-robed body squeezed with difficulty into Annette's tiny room and looked down at the basketful of kittens with a world of love and compassion in her large brown eyes. The heavy gold cross on her chest bobbed up and down and fell against the chest of drawers with a clatter.

'Och, the bonny wee kit-cats!' said Sister Marie Theresa, whose mother had been a Scot and whose real name was Kirsty. 'Their eyes are all open now. Have they been fed or are you just going to do it now? If you're in a hurry, Annette, I can feed them for you.'

Annette *was* in a hurry, as always – she mustn't be late for rehearsal again – so she left sister Marie Theresa, who was secretly very pleased, feeding the kittens with the three little bottles, and snatched up her dancing things.

Thank goodness for nuns, she thought as she

hurried downstairs again, they're so dependable. Tomorrow was Ash Wednesday, she remembered, the beginning of Lent, and there would be so many services that scarcely a nun would be seen until Easter! Bells would be ringing calling them to prayer all day long – and often at outrageously early hours in the morning when people, like tired ballet-dancers, for instance, wanted to sleep. There had been times when Annette felt she'd have liked to muzzle those everlasting bells! But now, when she thought of Sister Marie Theresa patiently feeding her foundlings upstairs, she felt she would never grumble at the bells again.

3   ON TOUR

That night Monsieur Georges died, and Miss Marty took over the Cosmopolitan School of Ballet.

For most young dancers there comes a time in his or her life when things look black, and this came to Annette now. She tried her best, but she made a bad job of it. Warm-hearted, temperamental, she had to have someone to dance for – some star to which to hitch her wagon, and now her star had fallen.

'I can't dance – I'm too miserable!' she said to her reflection in the tiny mirror above her chest-of-drawers. And her reflection looked back at her, white-faced and sad-eyed, and repeated, 'I can't dance when I'm miserable.' It was true, in Annette's case anyway. She had loved Monsieur Georges with every fibre of her being. He was like the sunlight to her, and now that he was gone she was like a bird, shut away from the light, which could no longer sing.

When Annette had refused the offer of Mr Solomon Isaacs, the world-famous film producer, to go to Hollywood, and had thrown in her lot with the

Cosmopolitan Ballet, all had gone well with her for a short time. She had danced the chief role in *The Little Matchgirl*, the ballet that Monsieur Georges had choreographed especially for her, though she didn't know it, and the Georges Reinholt ballet-school had won the Cecchetti Casket. Then she had joined the company, and had worked away in the corps de ballet, but always with the knowledge that Monsieur Georges was watching her, was approving her efforts to improve herself and, when she found herself in difficulty, helping her. She might be only in the corps de ballet, or standing in the wings watching others more experienced than herself dance the leading roles, but she knew quite certainly that one day she would no longer be just a dancer in the wings; she herself would dance Odette-Odile, Aurora in *The Sleeping Beauty*, and all the rest of the great classical roles. But now, with Marion Marty in command, she felt she was in the back row of the corps de ballet because Miss Marty thought she belonged there, and would never be good enough to be anywhere else.

She slept badly too. Her dreams were haunted by the tragedy that had befallen her hero. She dreamed she was wandering about in a hospital or in headlong flight down endless corridors. Sometimes she thought she was shut in a cage like a bird, and when she beat her hands against the bars, trying to escape, she woke up crying. Occasionally, very occasionally, her dream was a happy one. She thought she was in a

class taken by Monsieur Georges, and he was showing her how to do entrechats *six*. When she woke up
and found it wasn't true she shut her eyes again and
tried to go on dreaming . . .

Although the Cosmopolitan Theatre was the company's London home, the ballet had to spend a good
deal of its time on tour so that the theatre could be let
out to visiting companies who paid well for the hire
of it. Only in this way could the company make ends
meet. At present a group of Japanese dancers was

holding a four weeks' season in the theatre, while the real owners were rehearsing their new ballets in the roof studio, in preparation for their forthcoming tour of industrial towns in the Midlands, starting at Leeds and ending at Liverpool.

As the weeks went by, and summer came, Annette thought she had never been on such a depressing tour. Perhaps part of it was due to her own state of mind, but the towns they visited seemed to be especially drab, and the theatres more cold and noisy than the general rule. Far from dancing a leading role, she had scarcely even been given a solo the whole time, not even at a matinée – Marion Marty had seen to that! Even the Sugar Plum Fairy's solo which was Annette's pride had been given to Paddy. Paddy herself was very apologetic about it.

'I know you do it better than me, Annette, but there you are! Even if I refused to dance it, which one can't, it wouldn't do you any good. She'd only give it to someone else, and then she'd have her knife into me, so she would! As a matter of fact, you know, the company hasn't been an outstanding success on this tour. We haven't had a single full house so far, have you noticed? Not even on Saturdays. It's my opinion it's partly due to Simonetta. She doesn't like these Yorkshire and Lancashire people and doesn't consider them worth dancing for, and well they know it! They'd have liked you better, Annette mavourneen, even though you aren't so brilliant.'

And now it was Monday morning, and here they

were at Liverpool for a single matinée performance for children, at a small theatre near the quayside, their evening engagement having fallen through at the last moment. They had had a chapter of accidents the day before. They'd travelled on the Sunday, of course, like all theatrical companies, and one thing after another had delayed them. When they finally piled out of their four compartments at Liverpool it was nearly ten o'clock, and *then* they'd had to find their digs. After this had been done it was too late for Annette to ring up her mother as she did every Sunday night. Naturally Mrs Dancy couldn't ring Annette up, as she never knew where she was when on tour. And so we find Annette sitting on a seat on Mersey quayside, wondering whether or not she ought to wait until tonight to ring up at the cheap rate, or do it now on the standard. Common sense said, 'Wait until tonight, of course,' but Annette was a creature of impulse, and was never ruled by her head.

Of course, she thought, if I wait until twelve o'clock, she's sure to be in, because she starts to see about the lunch then and, after all, it's only half an hour.

Down she sat again, and while she waited she made her plans. The depressing tour was almost at an end, and tomorrow she would begin a fortnight's holiday. She would be able to go back to Dancing Peel and see her mother and all her friends. That was partly what she wanted to ring up about – her mother would want to know which train she was travelling by, so that they could meet her. She was sure Mr MacCrimmon, the vicar, would bring Mrs Dancy to the station in his car, since the buses were few and far between at Mintlaw. Perhaps Angus, Mr MacCrimmon's son, and a great friend of Annette's, would be there too. The last time Annette had talked to her mother on the telephone she had said that Angus had left school, and was going to start his new job any time now, but she hadn't said what the job was. At least, she had just begun to tell Annette when the money ran out and she had had to stop. It was most aggravating!

Her mother had sounded very happy, she thought, and of course there was no doubt about it, things had improved for the Dancy family now that she and her brother Maximilian had begun to earn their own living. They'd been able to help quite a lot – Max especially. Spanish dancing companies, it seemed, paid their dancers better than the ordinary ones – better than the Cosmopolitan Ballet Company anyway, thought Annette with a rueful twist of her lips. And then, since their home, Dancing Peel, had been divided, there had only been half the work to do. Mr MacCrimmon, who lived in the other half of the peel, shared Bella's services with Mrs Dancy – Mrs Dancy the mornings, himself the afternoons – and so Mrs Dancy had no heavy work to do at all. When Annette heard all this on the phone, or read about it in her mother's letters, which, when she was on tour, followed her round, so that she got them up to a week late, she felt less guilty about giving up the film career she had been offered. It was quite clear that at all events her beloved mother was happy, even though she wasn't accompanying her daughter round the United States of America, and that was all that mattered. Mrs Dancy had told Annette she was glad not to be going to America, as a matter of fact. There were several reasons for this, and one very special one which she might tell Annette in the not very distant future. It all depended – and then the money had run out again.

That had been the Sunday before last, and since then Annette had only had one letter sent on to her from the convent home, and it hadn't mentioned any special reason why Mrs Dancy was glad *not* to be going to America.

I expect she forgot to tell me, thought Annette. Or perhaps it was because she didn't want to leave her chickens – she always gets some week-old chicks about now. She glanced down at her watch, and saw that twenty minutes had slipped by. And that makes it ten to twelve. I'll risk it now, she decided, and sped across the road to the phone box.

'Hello, Mummy! It's me, Annette . . . Oh' (in disappointment) 'it's *not* Mummy.' The deep, rumbling tones certainly didn't belong to Mrs Dancy. Even on the telephone Annette recognised them as those of Bella. 'Well, where is Mummy? Is she still busy with the chickens? I thought she'd be sure – She's *what*? I can't hear you very well, Bella.

I thought for a moment you said *married*!'

'Aye, so I did,' said the deep voice at the other end of the line. 'Marret I said, and marret I meant. Yer mam's been and got hitched.'

'Hitched?' repeated the horrified Annette. 'Hitched to whom?'

'To the vicar. Who else?'

'The vicar? You mean Mr MacCrimmon? I can't believe it!'

'We all thinks – in the village, like – that she's done the right thing.' Bella's voice sounded slightly disapproving. She wouldn't let anyone criticise the mistress – not even Miss Annette. 'We all saw as how she was struck on the vicar – '

'*Bella!*' Now it was Annette's turn to sound disapproving.

'Oh, aye, and he was fair struck on her too,' observed Bella. 'But there was nawt odd aboot that. A right canny body is the mistress.'

'But why didn't she let me know?' demanded Annette. 'I just can't believe she'd do such a thing without telling me. After all, I *am* her daughter.'

'She tried to ring ye up, Miss Annette, hinny,' said Bella. 'But she couldna get through to ye. They said ye was awa', and no address left. She's writ ye a lang letter, sayin' as how she, and the vicar a'course, will look ye up i' Lunnon on their way back from their honeymoon.'

'*Honeymoon!*' Annette was almost too horrified to say the word.

38

'Aye – it's usual for folk like the mistress and the vicar to gan awa' for a bit holiday on their ain when they gets hitched up,' said Bella reasonably.

'Is Angus there, Bella? I mean, is he at Mintlaw?'

'Nay, Miss Annette. He's awa' to that bit island he's that struck on.'

'You mean he's in Skye?'

'Aye, that's the name,' said Bella. 'I remember it because it was that outlandish-like. As soon as ivor he'd seed his pa hitched, he was awa'.'

'But *where* in Skye?' demanded Annette.

'Noo I canna tell ye that, Miss Annette.'

'Oh, Bella, please think,' begged Annette. 'It's so very important.'

'It's nevor a bit o' good ma deein' that, Miss Annette, hinny,' came Bella's gruff voice, 'for it comes to me mind as how I nevor knew the name o' the place onyways.'

They said their farewells and Annette stood for a moment, quite still, while the world swung round her. Her mother married! Oh, no – she couldn't believe it! Yet she knew in her heart that it was true. Little things came into her mind: how young and pretty her mother had looked of late, and of course she was only just over forty and some people mightn't think that so very old. And then she remembered how Mr MacCrimmon had seemed to love doing things for Mrs Dancy – things like carrying the water and the coal; making things easier for her.

And that's what Mummy meant when she wrote and said she might tell me a very special reason why she was glad she wasn't going over to America. Of course! I might have guessed!

4   OH, FOR A WHITE SHIP!

Annette walked slowly back to her seat and flopped on it. In those brief six minutes since she had left it last, her life had changed. No longer was her beloved mother her own special property. She belonged to someone else now – Angus's father! And Angus himself? Why, Angus was now her brother – well, anyway, sort of!

Sitting there, Annette began to think of Angus, and the more she thought about him the more she longed to see him and talk to him. Angus was so wise. She wondered if he had guessed what was going on – if he knew that his father and her mother . . . Yes, she wouldn't be a bit surprised if Angus knew all the time, and had told no one. Oh, if only Angus were here to talk to. But he was in Skye. He couldn't be much farther away!

She got up and began walking along the quayside. It was a lovely June day, and the air was full of the mewing of seagulls as they wheeled overhead. It was a day full of light and sunshine – the sort of day when nobody ought to be unhappy. The little tug-boats had been newly painted, and there were several yachts dancing on the water as if in delight.

Oh, for a sail in one of them, thought Annette enviously. Or even a quite ordinary ship would do. How lovely to sail away and leave one's sorrows behind! I think I'd choose that white ship over there – she looks friendly. 'What's her name?' she asked a sailor who, seated on a sort of platform, was painting the hull of a very rusty cargo boat. 'And where is she going to?'

'Over the sea to Skye, ducks,' said the man promptly. 'Like the song says! She's called the *Flora MacDonald*, and she sails on the evenin' tide.'

Annette could hardly believe her ears. Skye! Just when she'd been thinking about it! A thought came into her mind. What if she went to Skye for her fortnight's holiday. If she couldn't go home, and it certainly didn't seem any use her going there now, where better than Skye? She was pretty sure that Angus would be staying with his friend Jaimie Gordon, the laird of Airdrochnish, and she could stay there too. Jaimie, like all Highlanders, was the soul of hospitality and would welcome her at Airdrochan Castle, she knew. Then her heart sank. She hadn't enough money for the ticket. She always sent half her salary home to her mother to help with the house-keeping, only holding back enough for her own digs and pocket money. She had enough for her fare home to Northumberland – one way – and that was all. It was twice as far and more to Skye, so it would cost a fantastic amount.

Disconsolately she turned her back on the white ship and began to walk back in the direction of the town. She'd have to get something to eat somewhere, she supposed, though she didn't feel hungry. The sailor shouted after her:

'All the info in that winder!' He waved to a building opposite. 'Summer Cruises to the Western Isles.'

Annette hesitated and was lost. It wouldn't do any

harm just to *look*, would it? She could perhaps get a brochure telling her all about it, and it would be lovely just to read the names of the places – lovely soft-sounding names like Arisaig, and Loch Nevis and Sheildaig.

She crossed the road to the building. A tremendous idea had swum into her brain – an idea so staggering it didn't bear thinking about. She must act before she thought, or she'd take fright. She walked into the office. It was quite bare, except for a counter covered with brochures, and a model of a small white ship mounted upon a plinth of pale-green Iona stone. A large picture of the same ship hung on the wall opposite the door. There was no one behind the counter, but standing, arms folded behind his back, apparently deep in contemplation of the picture, stood a young man dressed in naval uniform, with rings of gold braid round his sleeves, and WEST WATER CRUISES above in gold letters. On the counter lay a peaked cap with the same magic words round the band. He turned as Annette pushed open the door, and looked at her in an interrogatory manner.

'Well, lassie?' he said in a pleasant Scottish voice. 'And what can I be doing for you?'

'I've come about the *Flora MacDonald*,' Annette said breathlessly before she lost her courage. 'Are you anything to do with her?'

'I'm the purser,' said the uniformed man. 'Are you wishing to make an inquiry? As far as I know the ship is fully booked up to the middle of September. After that date, there may be a few berths. The clerk is out at the moment, but if I can be of any help – '

'Oh, you *can*,' said Annette eagerly. 'I mean, if you're the purser. Pursers are awfully important people, aren't they – all that money!'

The purser felt his heart warm towards the girl. A nice wee lassie, he thought her. She knew what was what!

'It's like this, you see,' went on Annette. 'I want to go to the Island of Skye, and I see that you – I mean, of course, *she*,' she nodded at the picture of the *Flora MacDonald*, 'is going there. The awkward part of it is that I've got no money – at least, not nearly enough to get me there, even by train, and of course cruises are *much* more expensive, aren't they? So I thought that perhaps – ' she rushed on before her courage failed her ' – I thought perhaps you might give me a job.'

'Er – what kind of a job?' the purser asked at length, and got the shock of life when she answered:

'I could dance for you – ballet, I mean. I'm a dancer, you know, and being professional I expect I should do it better than the passengers.'

The purser could well believe it! How many dismal so-called talent concerts had he compered!

'But how do I know you can dance?' he asked unnecessarily, since it didn't need more than half an eye to see that the child, and now that he looked at her more closely, he saw that she was older than he had thought at first, was telling the truth. Her every graceful movement proclaimed her to be indeed a dancer. 'Have you anything to prove it?'

For answer Annette dropped her old mackintosh down upon the parquet floor, kicked off her shoes, and gave him the Odette solo from *Swan Lake*. Then she put her shoes on again, and gave him a vivacious little Spanish dance that she made up on the spot.

'My brother Max is a Spanish dancer with Teresa and Luisillo,' she told the fascinated purser. 'So I've learned quite a lot of zapateado and castanet-playing from him.'

'Yes, I can see that you can dance,' he said when she had finished. 'But what company are you with, and how is it that you can think of going on a cruise – if you don't mind my asking?'

'Oh, no, I don't mind at all,' said Annette politely. 'I'm a member of the Cosmopolitan Ballet Company, and we've just been given a fortnight's holiday. I *was* going home, but my mother suddenly decided to get married again. I've only just heard about it,' she added, 'over the telephone. I may say it was a frightful shock!'

'I can well imagine that,' said the purser. 'Unless, of course, you knew about it beforehand.'

'I hadn't an idea,' said Annette. 'Well, now you see how it is that I can't go home. It's because my mother is on her honeymoon. So I had a notion to go to Skye instead. I have several friends there.'

'I see,' said the purser gravely.

'Oh, and besides being a dancer, I was once a film star. Honestly! I'm not having you on. I danced the leading role in the ballet sequences of the film *Pride o' the North*. Here's the contract, signed by my dear Mr Goldberg himself.' Out of the front of her jumper, Annette pulled a crumpled piece of paper. 'I keep it as a souvenir, to remind me that I *could* have gone to Hollywood if I'd wished. Sometimes,' her eyes became troubled, 'I feel I've made a mistake, and that I ought to have gone.'

The purser glanced from the crumpled document to Annette. She was telling the truth, so she was! To

47

DANCER IN THE WINGS

think that she had danced in the film *Pride o' the North!* Why, they'd shown it in the ship's lounge the cruise before last! As for Stanley Goldberg – he was a world-famous film producer. He ran a finger round his collar, and coughed.

'Er – Miss . . . ?'

'Dancy,' said Annette promptly. 'Annette Dancy.'

'Well, Miss Dancy, I'm afraid that your terms –'

'Oh, but I haven't any,' put in Annette. 'I mean, not what you would call terms in the ordinary sense. That's just the point. You see, I'm only sixteen, and until I'm eighteen I haven't a halfpenny. They put it all in the bank for me. So *terms* are no use at all for me. It's like this: if you'll let me sail in your ship as far as the Island of Skye, I'll dance for you – I mean your passengers – every evening if it's wet. Of course I'll be delighted to dance if it isn't wet,' she added eagerly, 'only I don't expect they'll want me to.'

Won't they! thought the purser. He could just imagine the sensation the child was going to make aboard the *Flora MacDonald*. He could see it in headlines in all the Scottish newspapers: FILM STAR ENTERTAINS PASSENGERS OF WEST WATER CRUISES.

Then he grew cautious.

'You're sure you're allowed to do it, Miss er – Dancy? I mean, does your present contract allow it?'

'Yes, of course I'm sure,' said Annette impatiently. 'There's nothing in my contract to say that I mustn't dance on board ship. And anyway, I'm not getting any money for it, so no one could object. If you could decide quickly, Mr er . . . ?'

'McPherson.'

'Well, Mr McPherson, if you could just make up your mind whether you want me or not, I'd be ever so grateful. You see, it's my lunch-time, and I get so hungry. Ballet dancers are terribly hungry people.'

'Very well,' said the purser. 'It's a go! Mind you,' he added, 'you'll have to share a cabin with two other people. You don't mind?'

'Oh, no, why should I?' said Annette. 'I often share digs with people. What time does your ship sail?'

'She sails with the evening tide,' said the purser.

'Yes, I know – a sailor told me that, but what time does the tide ebb, or flow, or whatever it is?'

The purser smiled at her ignorance.

'Passengers go aboard at five. She sails at six prompt . . . Wait a minute. You'll be wanting your ticket.' He made one out for her on the spot, and handed it over.

Annette took it, and did a delighted entrechat on the spot. She was so thrilled, she could hardly stop herself from turning a pirouette as well. She had forgotten all about the bombshell of her mother's marriage. Annette was like that – in the depths of despair one minute, and on top of the world the next.

'Goodbye, Mr Purser,' she said, her hand on the doorknob. Then she took it off again, and came back to the counter. 'There's only one thing – '

'What's that?'

'I have a performance this afternoon. It's for children, and it's in the Central Hall, down in Deansgate. It ought to be finished by five. You *will* let me aboard if I'm a bit late?'

'I'll see to it,' promised the purser gravely. 'But not a moment after six, mind you. She sails with the evening tide.'

'I'll be there,' Annette said, and skipped out.

5   THE *FLORA MACDONALD*

After a cup of coffee and a couple of sandwiches at the nearest snack-bar Annette sped home to find Paddy sitting on the bed darning a new pair of point-shoes. Into her friend's envious ears she poured the tale of her morning's adventures. When she had finished, Paddy wasn't quite sure who had married who, but one fact stood out quite clearly – Annette had got a job as Entertainer on board ship, and was going to Skye. Yes, this very evening!

'You sure have all the luck of the Irish, Annette mavourneen, in spite of the fact that you haven't a drop of Irish blood in your veins!'

'Yes, I always did have dancer's luck,' said Annette, 'although these last few weeks I must say it seemed to have deserted me. But now, Paddy, it's a question of what I'm to wear. I can't take much, you know, because when I get to Skye I shall probably have to walk miles and miles.'

'You can have the loan of my string-bag,' offered Paddy. 'The one I keep for the left-outs.' This was what they called the things they forgot to pack. 'It will be wonderful, as long as it doesn't rain!'

'I'm afraid it always does rain in the Highlands!' laughed Annette. 'But never mind, I'm sure it will be better than anything *I* have.'

Finally they packed Annette's pyjamas, brush and comb, and toothbrush into the string-bag, together with two pairs of point-shoes, tights and a case of make-up.

'I can wear my old mackintosh,' said Annette, 'and you can take my new suit back to London with you, Paddy – if you wouldn't mind. I'm pretty sure I shan't need a suit on a cruise.'

After they had finished the packing they went out and bought a large quantity of stiff white muslin and a small quantity of satin, with which Annette declared she could make herself a classical tutu in no time at all.

'And how about cramming in my evening dress – the old net one,' said Paddy as an afterthought.

'Yes, that's a good idea,' said Annette, 'thank you most awfully. I was wondering what I could wear for my *La Sylphide* solo. I feel that *La Sylphide* will be a most suitable thing to dance when we get into Scottish waters, as it's a Scottish ballet.'

Paddy knew Annette so well by now that it didn't surprise her in the least that her friend was thinking solely about her ballet dresses and not at all about what she was going to wear herself in the evening aboard the *Flora MacDonald*.

And so it was that at exactly five minutes to six a

small girl in an ancient mackintosh, with a bulging string-bag over her shoulder, accompanied by a bigger girl carrying a large brown-paper parcel, ran full-tilt up the quayside where the *Flora MacDonald* was berthed.

'Goodbye, Annette, me darlin'',' cried the larger girl, handing over the parcel. 'Take care of yourself, and give my love to Skye. Sure and I wish I was coming with you, so I do!'

'Goodbye, darling Paddy!' cried Annette, pausing in the middle of the gangway and pushing back a coil of springy white net that was escaping from the parcel. 'I wish you were too! And thank you for the loan of the evening dress, and for coming to see me off . . . Goodbye! Oh, and Paddy, I nearly forgot – would you please send on any letters that come for me. There will be one from my mother, and it's *most* important . . . Oh, but where will you send it to?'

'Oban, miss,' put in one of the sailors helpfully.

'Oban, Paddy!' cried Annette in her clear voice.

'Sure, and I'll not forget,' came Paddy's voice from the quayside.

Just at this moment the ship's siren blew, the gangway was removed with a clatter, and the ceremony of raising the anchor began. Annette was so fascinated by the sight of the chief engineer directing operations from the bows, and by the noise the chains made as they rushed round the winch, not to mention the seaweedy anchor coming up from the depths of Liverpool's mud, that she nearly forgot to wave a final goodbye to Paddy on the quayside.

A nudge on her arm made Annette jump. A sailor had picked up her string-bag in one hand and tucked the bulging parcel under his arm.

'Want to see your cabin, miss?' he asked.

'Oh – er, yes, I expect I ought to,' answered Annette. She didn't want to really. She wanted to stay and watch the blurred grey mass that was Liverpool disappear into the blue distance; she wanted to feel the fresh sea breeze in her hair, and the 'spring' of the ship under her feet. But she supposed she ought at least to know where her cabin was, so she followed the man below.

It was quite a large cabin, compared with those Annette had caught a glimpse of on her way down. It had a row of three portholes down one side, with a long sofa underneath and a sort of broad windowsill above, which, judging by the strip of mirror, was meant to do duty for a dressing-table. There were two bunks, one above the other, and it was obvious that the sofa turned into a bed at night. Apart from a large wardrobe and three small chairs, there was no other furniture. She peeped into the wardrobe and found it full to bursting point with summer clothes, most of them brand new, and several evening dresses. There was also a fancy-dress costume – an eighteenth-century lady, by the look of it – which took up a lot of room.

Where am I going to put my ballet-dress – when I've made it? was Annette's thought as she closed the door of the wardrobe, not without difficulty. Then she saw with relief that there were several hooks on the back of the door, and also between the portholes. Thank goodness! Her precious ballet dress would at least be hung up, even if all her other clothes lay on the floor!

She ran over to the nearest porthole, opened it and pushed out her head. To her left rushed a miniature

Niagara Falls of yellowish white water. Then she raised her eyes from the water and saw that they had come to the end of the shipping lane, and were really out in the open sea.

She was so busy leaning out of the porthole and trying not to miss anything that she didn't hear the cabin door open. A loud cough made her draw in her head so quickly that she bumped it on the side of the small aperture. The cabin seemed to be full of people, though after a few moments she saw that there were only three – an exceedingly glamorous female in navy slacks and a nautical jersey, an older woman, and a tall girl of about sixteen who, with her long thin neck, long thin legs and a striped dress that accentuated the general thinness, instantly made Annette think of a giraffe.

'What are you doing in our cabin, little girl?' demanded the older woman in a loud, rather hectoring voice that sounded as if she were well used to giving orders. 'Are you being sick?'

Annette was so astonished that for a moment she said nothing, then she exclaimed, 'Sick? Good gracious, no! Why, I never thought about it.'

'You wait until we round the Mull of Kintyre!' put in the thin girl. 'We'll probably all be sick!'

'If you're not being sick,' went on the older woman, 'what, may I ask, are you doing in our cabin?'

Her cabin, indeed, thought Annette. Okay, let her have it!

'This is my cabin,' she said brightly. 'But if, as you

56

say, it's your cabin too, perhaps we're going to share it. Though I can't see – ' looking round ' – where we're all going to sleep – unless of course,' she added, 'I share a bunk with one of you.'

'Indeed, no!' said the other, horrified. 'I never heard of such a thing. My name, by the way, is Hepple – Miss Hepple – and this is my niece, Janet, and this – ' indicating the glamorous female ' – is Miss Gilda Akenside. We book this cabin every year for our cruise because it's so commodious and quiet.' Since the noise at that moment was so deafening that she had to shout to make herself heard, Annette had every excuse to look bewildered.

'My aunt means,' explained Janet, 'that, although it's noisy just now, and will be tonight, as well, because we don't anchor anywhere on the first night, it will be nice and quiet after that – except of course for the dynamos,' she added. 'And as they're on the other side of the ship, they don't disturb us much. This cabin is one of the best, if not *the* best, in the ship. You should just see those on the bridge deck – they're so tiny you couldn't swing a mouse in them, let alone a cat! They haven't any wardrobes either. Those on the promenade deck aren't much bigger.'

'Janet, you talk far too much,' broke in Miss Hepple. 'If you were in my class, I should deal very severely with that runaway tongue of yours.' (Ah! thought Annette. Schoolmistress!) 'I'm still waiting to hear, little girl, what you are doing in our cabin? I cannot believe that it is yours too. The purser would never do such a thing. He's a great friend of mine.'

'And mine too,' said Annette promptly. 'I think he's one of the very nicest men I know. He told me I should have to share a cabin, and asked if I minded, and I said no, I was used to sharing digs with all sorts of peculiar people. Not,' she added hastily, 'that you're at all peculiar, Miss Hepple, but you know what I mean . . . I wonder what that is?' She had caught sight of a long, rectangular slab of wood let into the wall by the side of the wardrobe. It had two handles that rattled and added to the general noise.

'We don't know,' said Janet in blood-curdling tones. 'I say it's a coffin – in case anybody dies out at sea, you know, and you have to put them over the side. We've tried pulling the handles, but it seems to be locked.'

At this moment there was a knock on the door, and a cabin steward appeared. With an 'Excuse me, ladies!' he strode over to the 'coffin', inserted a key in the keyhole, pulled at the handles, and down came a folding bed, complete with bedding.

'Well, now we know!' laughed Annette. 'It's evidently a bed – my bed.'

'I simply can't believe it,' Miss Hepple kept saying. 'We've had this cabin for four, no five, years running, and there have only been the three of us in it.'

'I'm awfully sorry,' apologised Annette. 'I'll try not to disturb you. I shall be sewing most of the day – at first, anyway. You see, I have two ballet-dresses to make.'

'Ballet-dresses?' echoed the glamorous blonde, who hadn't spoken so far. 'What on earth do you want to make ballet-dresses for? If it's the fancy dress ball you're thinking of, I warn you lots of people go as ballet-dancers. They're dreadfully common!' Although the cabin was stiflingly hot, Annette could feel a chill creeping through it.

'Oh, but of course you don't know about me,' said Annette. 'I'm going to entertain the passengers on this cruise.'

'Entertain the passengers?' echoed Miss Akenside. 'How quite ridiculous! Why, whatever could a child like you do to entertain anybody?'

'I can dance,' said Annette, nettled. 'I'm a dancer by profession, though I'm on holiday just now. And, as a matter of fact, I danced in a film once, and if I'd liked I could have been a film star – though I expect you wouldn't believe it,' she added. Annette had no false illusions about her general appearance offstage.

'No, I certainly wouldn't believe it,' said Gilda Akenside bluntly.

Annette didn't bother to pull out the contract to convince her. After all, what did it matter anyway? She probably wouldn't understand a word of it. All this time she herself had been very busy unpacking the string-bag and stowing away her few belongings in the drawer that had appeared with the unfolding of the bed. Her evening dress, or rather Paddy's, she hung on one of the hooks beside the nearest porthole, where it swung to and fro looking like an exotic

curtain. Then she snapped the string round the
brown paper parcel, whereupon out oozed great
waves and sheaves of white ballet net and satin.

'Oh, it will make the most gorgeous dress!' said
Annette, lost in admiration at the sight. 'If I start on it
now, I'll have it finished by tomorrow, and I'll be able
to make my first appearance in the evening after
dinner.'

The two women, after taking one disapproving
look at the mass of net which was expanding every

minute, and consequently taking up more and more space, had gone out of the cabin, slamming the door behind them. Since the engines were making such a noise, the slam was robbed of most of its effect.

'Oh, dear, I do hope they weren't too annoyed,' said Annette to Janet, who had stayed behind and was watching the proceedings with interest. 'But one has to ply one's profession, hasn't one?' She promptly took out her nail scissors and proceeded to cut the net.

There was a short silence, then Janet said slowly, 'She's not such an awful old hag as you might think – Aunt Phoebe, I mean. She's not my aunt really, but I call her that for convenience. You see, my mother is a widow, so we're pretty hard up, and if it wasn't for Aunt Phoebe I shouldn't get a holiday at all. She's a teacher at a school in our town – Bolton, near Manchester. Thank goodness it isn't my school! I don't think I could stand that, although, as I say, she is good to me in her way – '

'But if she's a schoolteacher, how can she come on a cruise now?' asked Annette, taking a couple of pins out of her mouth, and then sitting back on her heels and looking up at Janet with grave, dark eyes. 'It's not the summer holidays yet.'

'No; but I expect you've heard of the Wakes?' said Janet. Then, as Annette looked puzzled, she explained. 'It's a sort of religious thing the Cotton Towns have every year, and there are lots of processions, and everyone joins in, and they call it 'walking'. Well, we all have a holiday, so Aunt Phoebe takes me on this cruise. Miss Akenside comes too. She's in a dress shop, and of course it's shut too for Wakes Week. She's a proper old hag, is Gilda Akenside, although I suppose "hag" is the wrong word because she's not so old really – only about twenty-five. Miss Akenside thinks she owns the blessed ship, and then you come along. It's no wonder she's jealous!'

'Jealous?' echoed Annette. 'Who of? You don't mean me?'

Janet nodded.

'Yes. You see, the purser always arranges a talent concert, and all the people who can sing or dance, or think they can, entertain their fellow pasengers. Judging by the yawns and coughs, I think most of the poor things are bored stiff, but Gilda Akenside doesn't care about that. She dances herself, you know – musical comedy stuff that she learns one night a week. Then of course there's the fancy dress parade. All the costumes are supposed to be made on board ship, but Gilda brings a real slap-up fancy dress with her. Last year she was a Seagull, with hundreds of feathers sewn on, and a real pair of wings, and of course she won the first prize. She always does.'

'But what about all the feathers?' asked Annette.

'Oh, she said she collected them on deck in the early mornings,' said Janet, 'and of course no one could prove she hadn't. By the way, wouldn't you get along faster with a rather bigger pair of scissors? I've got a big pair somewhere about. I always make my fancy dress on board.'

Annette accepted the scissors gratefully, and she and Janet very soon became fast friends. Annette told her new cabin-mate all about her home at Dancing Peel in Northumberland; her brother Max, who was a Spanish dancer with Teresa and Luisillo, and, last but not least, all about her own dancing career.

After half an hour's work, Janet holding the net and Annette cutting it, Annette straightened her back.

'Well, that's the end of that! Now for the frilling. Can you frill?'

Janet looked doubtful, so Annette explained.

'You have to start with an enormously long thread, because naturally you can't join it in the middle, or it wouldn't pull. If you start on one of the skirts, I'll run up the bodice and the lining. It must be lined, you see, to make it firm.'

And so Janet was initiated into the mysteries of making that most complicated of all articles of clothing – a classical tutu. It never occurred to Annette to ask whether her cabin-mate minded being roped in as assistant dressmaker. She herself couldn't imagine anyone in their right mind not wanting to make a ballet-dress. It's only fair to say that Janet was thrilled to associate herself with the ship's professional entertainer. It was a case of 'reflected glory' all right!

In a surprisingly short time the dress began to take shape.

'Of course, it ought to be cut all in one – the dress and the knickers, I mean,' said Annette with a little frown. 'But that's very difficult without a pattern, and I didn't have it with me in Liverpool. I certainly didn't expect I'd be needing it! So we must just make the dress and knickers separately, and then sew them together afterwards. By the way, I don't know your other name – your surname. Of course, it won't be Hepple, as Miss Hepple isn't your real aunt.'

'No, it's Maclean,' said Janet.

'Then you're Scottish?' cried Annette.

'Yes, but I've lived in Bolton all my life.'

'You haven't by any chance got a kilt with you?' asked Annette.

Janet nodded.

'Yes, but it's a frightfully old one. I only use it for messing about at home, and Mummy thought it would do for going ashore on wet days.'

'Do you think I might borrow it?' asked Annette. 'Just occasionally, I mean. Then I could give the passengers some Scottish dancing. Angus, he's a great friend of mine – in fact, he's really my brother now, since Mummy got married to his father – well, Angus taught me quite a lot of Scottish dancing. And Jaimie Gordon too. When we were in the film *Pride o' the North*, Jaimie and I used to practise together while they made up their minds which bit they were going to film.'

There was an awestruck silence.

'You really mean you were in that gorgeous film *Pride o' the North*?' said Janet. 'When you talked about being a film star to Aunt Phoebe I thought you were joking. And with Jaimie Gordon too! Gilda will be livid with envy. She's frightfully struck on him. I know for a fact she's been to see the film four times!'

'Then she must have seen me too,' said Annette, 'but of course she wouldn't remember me. Perhaps we'd better not mention the film – don't you think?'

'It might be better,' agreed Janet. 'But I'll lend you my kilt like a shot. It'll be too long for you, though.'

'Oh, I'll fold it over at the top,' laughed Annette. 'That's the best of being slim!'

6   AT SEA

Annette found that she and her cabin-mates were on the second sitting for meals. Janet changed into a summer dress, and Annette into a clean white blouse. Passengers could sit anywhere they liked on this first night, Janet explained, but after that their places would be arranged, and there they would sit for the rest of the cruise.

'All the terribly important people will be put at the captain's table,' she said. 'I see that Gilda has parked herself right next to him tonight. Oh, good! The purser's coming to sit at our table. I like him. Hello, Mr McPherson!'

The purser greeted Janet as an old friend, and then he turned to Annette and asked her how she was enjoying her first evening aboard the *Flora Mac-Donald*, whether she found her cabin comfortable, and if she had everything she wanted.

'You know,' he said to the table in general, 'we've got a very important young person aboard this cruise.' He indicated Annette in her ancient skirt and crushed, if clean, blouse. 'She is a dancer as well as a film star, and she is going to entertain us on this voyage.'

The table listened politely, not knowing whether he was serious or not. Most of them decided he wasn't, and one stout Yorkshireman laughed heartily at the very idea. There was indeed every excuse for their not believing what they were told. Anything less like a dancer – let alone a glamorous film star – than Annette Dancy at that moment would have been hard to find!

During the night the wind freshened, and the ship began to roll. Annette was in that unhappy state of being too tired to sleep. Besides, now that all the excitement of the last few hours was past, she had time to think, and everything came back to her with a rush. She was too unhappy even to feel seasick. And when at last she fell asleep to dream she was back home at Dancing Peel . . .

'Annette! Annette! Are you awake! Oh, I feel so awful!'

'Oh, Janet, it's you!' said Annette reproachfully. 'Why did you wake me up just then? I was having such a wonderful dream!' She covered her face with the bedclothes, trying to shut out reality and stay in her dream. Then she woke up fully and remembered Janet's last words.

'Janet, are you really seasick? Is there anything I can do to help?' A moan from Janet was her only answer.

Annette switched on the light and looked across at her friend. Poor Janet was a pale-green colour and every time the ship rolled, she moaned. Aunt Phoebe slept on undisturbed, snoring loudly. On the sofa underneath the three portholes Gilda Akenside was moaning too.

'Would you like some water?' asked Annette, who, although miserable, wasn't feeling at all seasick herself.

There was no answer from either Janet or Gilda. After a few minutes, feeling that she could do nothing to help, she switched off the light and lay down again.

Next morning Annette woke to a rainwashed world. Outside the portholes raced a tumbled grey sea, and a sky equally grey. There was no land to be seen anywhere. All the other occupants of the cabin appeared to be asleep so, making as little noise as possible, Annette dressed and opened the cabin door. The ship was almost deserted, except for stewards and stewardesses hurrying to and fro, carrying early morning cups of tea, and basins and towels. Clinging to the ropes that acted as handrails, she climbed several flights of stairs and eventually found herself out on the sports deck, which was situated in the stern. A ray of watery sunlight fell upon a couple of seagulls sitting on the rail near her. The early morning mist was lifting, and through it Annette saw a curiously-shaped heap of rock.

'That's Ailsa Craig,' said a very old gentleman who had appeared at her elbow. 'If you come up here after breakfast you'll see Arran coming up on the port bow. Due at Ardrossan about eleven o'clock.' So saying he hobbled away, clinging to the ship's rail with one frail blue-veined hand, and a walking stick with the other. And then Annette was alone again, unless you could count the seagulls, who had evidently come to the conclusion that she was harmless, and had gone to sleep. Annette's spirits rose and she began to dance. She always danced to express her feelings, so now, on the gleaming wet deck, she danced a Highland fling – a Scottish dance seemed most appropriate under the the circumstances.

After a few minutes she stopped to get her breath. The two seagulls, who had watched her with half-shut eyes, took fright and flew away with their plaintive mewing cries.

'Very nice indeed!' said a pleasant Scottish voice behind her.

She turned and beheld an immensely tall young man with red hair and very blue eyes, standing on the steep companionway that led up to the boat deck. He wore the navy blue uniform of an officer of the *Flora MacDonald*, having several rows of gold braid round his sleeve.

'Oh, I didn't know anybody was watching!' exclaimed Annette. 'I was just keeping my hand in – or rather, my feet – and the deck was so inviting. It's a lovely morning, isn't it? Who are you?'

'The chief engineer, at your service!' said the red-haired young man. 'And may I ask your name?'

'Annette Dancy,' said Annette.

'How appropriate!' said the young man with a smile.

'What do you mean?'

'Dancy by name, and Dancy by nature!' The young man laughed. 'I gather you are the young lady who is to entertain us in the evenings? I've heard all about you from the purser.'

'He's an awfully nice man, isn't he?' said Annette warmly. 'He didn't take nearly as much convincing as I thought he would.'

'Convincing?' echoed the chief engineer.

70

'I mean that I really am a dancer. I don't look very much like one, you know, not in my everyday clothes. But just wait till I've finished making my new tutu – then you'll all see how I can dance!'

'You forget – I've already had that pleasure,' said the chief engineer.

'Oh, but I mean ballet. Of course, Scottish dancing is a form of ballet, it's true, and I love it; but after all, I am English, at least, half of me is, and no one can really execute a Scottish reel or a Highland fling properly except the Scots themselves. Angus says so.'

'Angus?' repeated the young man. 'Friend of yours?'

'Yes, and no,' said Annette. 'Angus is really my brother.'

'Oh, I see – your brother?' said the chief engineer with interest. 'Well, you can tell Angus from me that I dare to differ from him. Rarely have I seen my native dancing performed with so much spirit and technical excellency.'

'You do talk oddly,' observed Annette. 'But then all Scotsmen do – sort of old-fashioned and stately. Angus is just the same, and so is Jaimie.'

'Another brother?' queried the chief engineer.

'Oh, good gracious no!' exclaimed Annette, laughing at the thought. 'Jaimie is the laird of Airdrochnish, and a very great person. He played the lead in a film I was in a short time ago.'

By this time the chief engineer had come down

from his perch on the companionway, and was standing beside her on the sports deck, or perhaps towering over her would be more accurate!

'If you have quite recovered your breath, Miss Dancy,' he said with a bow, 'would you favour me with the pleasure of the next dance?'

And so they danced on the wet deck – reels, flings and even a stately strathspey. One of the crew appeared, armed with an accordion, and accompanied them. Annette was nearly danced off her feet by that tall, red-headed Scottish engineer.

'Oh, that was lovely!' she said at length, collapsing against the rail. 'You're quite wonderful, your dancing, I mean,' she added hurriedly, because it wouldn't do for him to think she meant him! 'Well, there's the gong. I think I'd better go down to breakfast. Goodbye, Mr – er . . . ?'

'Hamish MacPhee,' said the chief engineer with a bow. 'Goodbye, Miss Dancy. Perhaps we may meet again.'

'I think you'd better call me just Annette, Mr MacPhee,' said Annette, regarding him with solemn dark eyes. 'Everyone does. Yes, I expect we shall meet again – a ship isn't a very big place, is it? But for most of today I shall be busy frilling in my cabin – making my new tutu,' she added, seeing that he looked puzzled. 'It must be finished in time for tonight, you see, because I want to start entertaining the passengers straight away, so as to earn my passage.'

'I quite understand,' said Hamish MacPhee solemnly. 'There's only one thing, if I may mention it. After lunch we anchor in Brodick Bay. You really ought to put aside the – er – frilling, and go ashore for an hour or two. Arran's a lovely island, and shouldn't be missed.'

'I'll think about it,' Annette promised, and off she ran, nearly having a head-on collision with Gilda Akenside who had just come up on deck and was looking anything but cheerful. She appeared to be seeking somebody, and when she saw the chief engineer she brushed past Annette, nearly flattening her against the rail, and dashed forward to intercept him. But Hamish MacPhee hadn't seen her, or perhaps didn't want to see her, for in three long strides he swung himself up the companionway on the boat deck, where the officers' quarters were, and disappeared.

'Oh!' said Gilda, her face falling. 'And I wanted to ask him what time we reached Arran.'

'After lunch,' said Annette promptly. 'He's just told me. He said I ought to go ashore, but I explained that I'd be frightfully busy with my tutu. All the same, I think that perhaps he's right, and it's an island that oughtn't to be missed. He's a wonderful dancer, isn't he? Scottish dancing, I mean.'

She wondered why the other girl turned her back abruptly and didn't answer. It certainly never occurred to Annette that Gilda Akenside, in regarding the *Flora MacDonald* as her own property, included the chief engineer!

7   THE ISLE OF ARRAN

At breakfast time the tables were almost empty, but at lunch nobody was missing. For one thing the sun had come out, the sea calmed down considerably and, last but not least, the magical Isle of Arran had appeared on the port bow. The purser announced over the loudspeaker that there would be a service of launches to and from the shore, the first one leaving at one o'clock, and the last at two. Annette was so busy with her frilling that she nearly missed the last launch, but she had the pleasant feeling that but for a few frills to be added to the knickers, and a few hooks and eyes, her dress was finished, ready to wear that very night. Janet had given her up for good, and had gone off with her aunt.

They landed at the little jetty in Brodick Bay, under the shadow of a dark mountain. The little village, clustered round a half-moon bay of glistening sand, glinted in the sun. Everything looked very clean and sparkling, as well it might after all the rain of the night before.

'Mind your step, lassie!' said the sailor helping Annette out of the boat on to the seaweedy jetty. 'It's a wee bit slippy!'

'Yes, we must take great care of our professional entertainer,' said a melodious Scottish voice, and out from behind a pile of lobster-pots, nets and other fishing gear stepped her friend of that morning – the chief engineer. 'I was beginning to think that your ballet dress was going to take pride of place over the romantic Isle of Arran!'

'I almost missed it,' admitted Annette; 'the last launch, I mean. It had actually started, but an awfully nice sailor saw me waving frantically from the top of the step-ladder down from the ship and came back for me.'

All this time they were walking down the jetty towards the village. Annette was wearing her old pleated skirt and ancient jumper, and her companion an equally ancient kilt topped by a fisherman's jersey that rippled round his neck like a large motor-car tyre. Over the jersey he wore a tweed jacket, much patched with leather at elbows and pockets, and smelling of peat and wood smoke. He carried an old mackintosh, strapped into a roll with a leather belt, slung over his shoulder.

'I thought of taking a walk up Glen Rosa – the loveliest glen in all Arran, and one of the bonniest in Scotland, I'm thinking,' he said as they left the jetty and set off along the white road. 'Could I persuade you to go too?'

Annette didn't need any persuading. She had never been to Arran, and had no idea what she ought to see, and no one to take her there if she had. She welcomed this red-haired young Scotsman who, although he had not the least claim to good looks, had something attractive about him, though it was impossible to define it. As for Hamish MacPhee – he was charmed by Annette's utter naturalness. She didn't giggle like most of the girls he met. She wasn't coy; nor did she try to flirt with him. Above all, he liked the grace of her every movement as she ran here, there and everywhere, delighted with everything she saw, from the tiny flowers that starred the emerald cushions of moss on the banks of the brawling mountain torrent that tumbled headlong down the glen, to the butterflies that sat sunning themselves, wings gently opening and shutting, on the long feathery grasses and warm lichened rocks.

They had left the road long since, and were now on the open moorland. They struck off up the steep hillside, higher and higher, until the *Flora Mac-Donald*, lying on the blue waters of Brodick Bay, looked like a child's toy sailing on a pond.

They sat down on a warm lichened rock, and ate a slab of chocolate the young man brought out of his pocket. After this, the chief engineer gathered a bunch of sweet-smelling mountain flowers and handed them to Annette, and it was at this moment that a strange thing happened. As they sat there on their rock the sun suddenly went in, and a cold

breath enveloped them. The white ship lying in Brodick Bay disappeared before their very eyes, and a swirling cloud of mist, seemingly coming from nowhere at all, swept over them, and in a moment or two had enfolded them in a cold, clammy, white shroud.

'Never mind,' said the chief engineer, 'we'll just sit here for a wee while, and it will lift in no time at all. It's best not to go moving about in a mountain mist.'

So they sat on their rock, and after a while Hamish MacPhee unrolled his mackintosh and put it round Annette's shoulders. They talked to pass away the time, and the young man learned all about Annette, her home in Northumberland and her ballet career.

Presently the young man began to look anxiously at his wristwatch. 'We must find our way down,' he said at length. 'The last launch leaves at seven o'clock. We must not miss it.'

And so they climbed down into the glen, slipping and sliding on the wet rocks. They dared not leave the stream for fear of going astray, but knew that as long as they followed the water they would come safely down in the end. Sometimes the going was very rough indeed, as well as very wet. When finally they reached level ground they were tired and out of breath. Annette was engulfed in the chief engineer's mackintosh, and he had tied a large silk handkerchief over her hair in a vain attempt to keep it dry. One of her cold wet hands was firmly clasped in his, and the other held the flowery nosegay. Together they raced along the road and down the jetty, where the last launch was just putting off for the ship.

'Hey!' shouted the chief engineer. 'Wait for us!'

Gilda, already seated in the launch, beheld them thus, and her heart burned with jealousy.

'Move over, please!' said the chief engineer in a tone of authority. Then he picked up Annette and swung her over the side, dropping her almost on Gilda's lap. 'Just made it! Got caught in the dickens of a mist up in Glen Rosa. Lucky we managed to get down in time!'

*　　*　　*

The first thing Annette did when they got back to the ship was to fill the wash-basin in her cabin with water and put her flowers in it. They would be lovely to wear in her hair later on.

That night she danced for them on deck. The mist had disappeared in that strange unaccountable way mists have in the Western Highlands, and there was a full moon sailing high in a cloudless star-studded sky. As a background for her dance she had the dark silhouette of Goat Fell, and at its foot the twinkling lights of Brodick village. She gave them first *La Sylphide*, dressed in Paddy's ballet-length evening dress with an overskirt of white net which floated in the night breeze. She wore a wreath of artificial flowers borrowed from Janet in her hair after all. When she had gone to her cabin after dinner to dress, she found that her bouquet of real flowers had disappeared.

'Oh, I threw them out of the porthole,' Gilda had said off-handedly when asked about them. 'I didn't know you wanted them, Annette.'

'You might at least have *asked* me,' Annette answered reproachfully.

'Well, you shouldn't have put them in the wash-basin — *our* wash-basin,' countered Gilda. 'How could I possibly wash in a basin full of flowers?'

'But you told me you always washed in the bath-room, because the basin in there is so much bigger,' argued Annette, 'and there's a mirror. You said so most distinctly.'

'Well, I changed my mind tonight,' snapped Gilda. 'And why all the fuss? They were dead anyway.'

Since nothing would bring the flowers back again, Annette, as we have said, wore the artifical ones. After her *La Sylphide* solo she gave them the Dance of the Sugar Plum Fairy, dressed in her new tutu. The chief engineer had fixed up a microphone which relayed the music from the lounge up to the sports deck. Everyone was there. Even the captain watched her from his bridge, and the cook and his mates came up from the galley and cheered.

8   THE MISCHIEF MAKER

They left Brodick Bay early next morning and by lunch-time were rounding the Mull of Kintyre. Fortunately the sea had calmed down somewhat, so nobody felt ill. As there was nothing to see Annette went below and spent some time ironing her ballet dresses. She had made friends with the cabin steward, and he had produced an iron and a board to do it on.

Later in the afternoon she went up on deck, where she was waylaid, first by Janet, who persuaded her to have a game of deck quoits, and then by two middle-aged women.

'Oh, Miss Dancy,' said the younger of the two, 'we saw you early yesterday morning out of our porthole, it looks out over the sports deck, you know. You were dancing with the chief engineer, Scottish dancing it was, and we wondered, Estelle and I, if you would – I mean, would it be an awful lot of trouble – '

'Alice means, would you be so kind as to show us how to do it sometime,' broke in the older. 'The eightsome reel, and the Gay Gordons, and perhaps that one called the Dashing White Sergeant. Such a lovely name, don't you think?'

'Of course I will,' promised Annette. 'I'll do it tonight. I'll get Mr MacPhee to round up a few more people, and we'll have a class. We could have it up here on the sports deck if it's fine, or in the card room if it isn't.'

'What a sweet little thing!' whispered the two women to each other as Annette went on her way.

As time passed most of the passengers in the *Flora MacDonald* grew to like Annette, and the crew openly adored her. They regarded her rather as a mascot. In the evening, after she had danced for the passengers, and had held her Scottish dancing class, she would go down to the galley and dance for the crew.

They spent their third day at sea sailing round the islands of Islay and Jura, and now their course was set for the Isle of Mull. Annette spent as short a time as she could in her cabin, for there was so much to see outside, but tights must be washed and dresses have to be pressed, and with Annette her ballet came first always – even before the scenery. However, her dresses were finished at last and hung up on pegs ready for that night's performance, and then there were only her tights. She washed them in the hand-basin at top speed and hung them in the open porthole to dry. She had made a tiny clothes-line out of a piece of string, and had begged a couple of

clothes-pegs from the friendly cabin steward. Being long, the tights floated out of the opening, but as it was an outside porthole and nobody could see them she decided it didn't matter.

'Someone from another ship could,' said Gilda, carefully outlining her lips with a lip-pencil and then filling in with lipstick.

'But there aren't any other ships,' said Annette.

'There might be,' argued Gilda.

'Oh, well if one appears I'll take them in,' promised Annette. So saying she hurried on deck to find that they were steaming up the Firth of Lorne towards Oban. She found a deckchair and, wrapping herself up in one of the ship's rugs, she put her feet up on the rail and prepared to relax and enjoy the scenery which was growing grander every minute. There were the hills of Mull on the port side, and a big mountain had appeared aft which she recognised as Ben Cruachan, the elderly gentleman having told her at lunch that she would see it unless the mist came down. She wasn't left alone for long, however. After a few minutes the chief engineer appeared at her elbow, saying he was off duty. He stood for a while talking to her in the sheltered alcove made by a couple of lifeboats. The sun had come out with a vengeance and it was really hot. Annette discarded the rug, and her cardigan too.

'What time do we reach Oban?' she asked the young man. 'And where does one pick up one's letters?'

He laughed.

'One doesn't! At least, not if they're addressed "C/o West Water Cruises". They'll be collected by the captain's launch and put in the letter rack outside the purser's office before dinner. Are you expecting a letter?'

'Oh, yes – from my mother, telling me all about her new marriage.'

'We tie up at Oban alongside the fish quay about three o'clock, so you have time for tea before going ashore. You can even catch the shops before they close.'

'Well, I don't really want to buy anything,' said Annette. 'Except a couple of postcards. I must send one to Angus at Airdrochan Castle to let him know I'm coming. The castle belongs to Jaimie Gordon, of course, but Angus always stays there.'

The chief engineer left her shortly after that, and disappeared into his cabin near by, but not before Gilda Akenside had seen him talking to Annette.

Returning to her cabin, she ran full tilt into Gilda, who was just coming out.

'Oh, sorry!' exclaimed Annette. 'I didn't see you. It's so dark down here after the sunlight on deck.' Then, as her eyes became used to the darkness, she noticed that Gilda was looking at her strangely. 'What's the matter? What are you looking at me like that for?'

Gilda didn't answer at once. She stepped aside to let Annette go into the cabin, then she followed and closed the door.

'Annette,' she began, 'I've got to tell you something, strictly in confidence, of course. People are talking about you.'

Annette's large brown eyes opened wide, though not with astonishment at being talked about. She was used to that. Film stars live under the public eye, and even dancers cannot altogether escape the blaze of publicity. No, what surprised Annette was Gilda's admitting it. And why sound so mysterious about it? Therefore Gilda's next words came as an even greater shock.

'Yes,' said Gilda, 'the whole ship's laughing at you, Annette Dancy.'

'Laughing at *me*?' Annette was getting more and more mystified. 'But what for?'

'The way you run after poor Mr MacPhee,' said

Gilda. 'I felt it my duty to tell you – for your own sake, I mean.'

Annette was so astonished, not to say horrified, that she couldn't speak for a moment.

'Running after Mr Macphee?' she said at length. 'You – you mean the chief engineer? You don't – you couldn't possibly mean . . . ' Words failed her.

'I mean it's a disgrace the way you chase after the poor man,' went on Gilda, all her grievances against Annette welling up. 'Getting him to take you up Glen Rosa . . . Disappearing into the mist – couldn't find the way down! What a story! D'you know what they say? They say you're just cheap – '

Annette couldn't bear any more. She pushed past Gilda, wrenched open the cabin door and fled. But

the corridor was full of the passengers who occupied the other cabins down on the main deck, all bent upon getting smartened up to go ashore, and she couldn't face them. She couldn't! She dashed into the bathroom, shut and bolted the door, then laid her hot forehead down upon the edge of the cool basin.

'How dreadful of me!' she moaned in an agony of shame and self-reproach. 'How dreadful!' Then she began to wonder – had she really done anything so very dreadful? *Had* she, in fact, run after the chief engineer? Wasn't it truer to say that he had run after her? She hadn't asked him to watch her dance that first morning – she hadn't known he existed. She hadn't known that he would turn up on the jetty at Brodick either, nor that he would come and talk to her today, though she supposed she had, quite unwittingly, parked her chair almost right outside his door! Well, it wouldn't happen again, she thought passionately. No one was going to say that Annette Dancy ran after young men! Cheap, indeed! The whole ship laughing at her, was it? She'd show them! The soul of honesty herself, Annette never for a moment doubted Gilda's word.

And so she set about avoiding the chief engineer as if he had the plague. She began at Oban by going ashore as soon as the gangway was lowered, knowing that he would certainly expect her to have tea first – everyone was well aware of Annette's appetite by this time! Every time the young man caught sight of her going into a shop and followed to have a word with her, she managed to slip out without meeting him. Once he ran her to earth in the chief confectioner's, where a queue of passengers from the *Flora MacDonald* were ordering boxes of shortbread to be sent home.

'Oh, hello, Annette,' he began. 'Where have you been all day? I've looked for you everywhere,'

'I'm sorry, Mr MacPhee,' said Annette with dignity, though her heart was beating wildly, 'but I've left a parcel in the cloakroom. I must go and fetch it.'

He waited patiently for her to return so that he could carry her parcel for her, but she did not re-appear. When he made inquiries of one of the shop girls, he was told, 'Och, yes, the lassie went out the other way. No, she had no parcel, unless it was a rare wee one and couldna be seen.'

The young man's feelings towards Annette began to change. Up to now he had no serious intentions towards the ship's professional dancer. He thought of her as 'a nice wee lassie'; had liked being with her, and talking with her, just as he liked being with and talking to dozens of other girls he met. But now, piqued and amazed by her behaviour, he began to think of her more seriously. If Gilda had wanted to make the chief engineer fall in love with Annette, she couldn't have gone a better way about it!

During that evening and most of the next day Annette and the chief engineer played at hide-and-seek all over the ship, and each time she slipped through his fingers he grew more determined to have it out with her; to find out what he had done to offend her; because, for the life of him, he couldn't think of anything. Not a single compliment had passed his lips. He couldn't have been more circumspect. Hamish MacPhee, angry and hurt, set himself out to corner Annette. She would tell him what was the matter between them, or he'd know the reason why!

9   IN TOBERMORY BAY

That evening, after cruising all day up lovely Loch Linnhe to Fort William and back again, they anchored in Tobermory Bay in the Island of Mull.

After dinner Annette went down to her cabin and read her mother's letter for the fifth time since she had received it the day before:

My darling,

I don't know what you will say when you know that I have decided to marry again! It's not that I have forgotten your dear father, or that I love him any the less, but that I am so very lonely living here all by myself now that my children have gone out into the world, and it appears that Malcolm was lonely too. Last night he asked me to marry him, and I have said 'yes', because I am very fond of him and deeply grateful for all the kind and thoughtful things he has done to help me since he came here as vicar – and especially since the peel was divided and we have shared it. It's true to say that I love him, but of course in quite a different way to the love I had for your dear father. I don't expect you to understand at the moment, Annette, you're very young for your age in many ways, but someday you will.

I have given you one or two hints as to how things were going, Annette darling, but you were never much of a one for hints, were you? Always thinking about your dancing! Of course I could not do more than hint, because I didn't know with certainty exactly how Malcolm felt towards me until last night.

We rang up the convent home to see if there was any possible means of getting in touch with you, but they didn't know your address. In fact, they knew even less than we did! So all I can do is write this letter, and we'll have an extra long phone call tomorrow night (Sunday) when you ring up.

Annette's tears came thick and fast when she read this, for of course she had spent Sunday in the train, so hadn't been able to make her usual phone call.

After the wedding – that is, Monday – Malcolm and I will fly over to Switzerland for our honeymoon. I've never flown before – in fact, I've never been out of England, so you can guess how thrilled I am!

Here Annette's tears flowed again. *She* had wanted to be the one to show her mother the world, and now Mr MacCrimmon – she refused to call him 'Father' – had got there first!

We are going to various places that Malcolm knows well, and of course he wants me to get to know them too, so we shall be away quite a long time. Three whole weeks! Never have I had such a holiday! In fact, I don't remember ever having a holiday at all.

There's only one fly in the ointment, as they say, and that's the fact that I can't see you and Max before we go, but we did manage to get in touch with Maxie yesterday, and he sent his best love and says he's sure we've done the right thing.

He *would*! thought Annette stormily. Boys are so thoughtless. They go off on their own affairs, and it doesn't matter to them *what* their mothers do! It didn't occur to her that that was exactly what she herself had done – gone off on her own affairs – and that perhaps Max, her brother, was taking a more unselfish and grown-up attitude than she was.

Angus has left school, as I told you before, and he will be here for the wedding. He's the dearest boy. I feel as if I had got two sons now! After the wedding he's going straight to Skye to join that friend of his – Jaimie Gordon. They plan to go to a place called Glen Brittle, which, so Malcolm tells me, is one of the best possible places for climbing the Cuillin Hills, and they're going to camp out there, and conduct parties of climbers (mostly undergraduates and schoolboys) up some of the difficult places. All very useful for Angus's job.

'She *still* doesn't tell me what sort of a job it is!' exclaimed Annette aloud. 'Oh, aren't letters maddening!'

On our way home we'll be sure to break our journey in London so as to see you, darling. We'll contact you from Paris or somewhere.
With all the love in the world from us both,
Mummy.

Oh, well, she thought, shrugging her shoulders, Annette Dancy was having a good holiday too, wasn't she? A whale of a time! In a few minutes, after she had changed, she'd be dancing again, with the romantic Tobermory Bay as her backcloth, and the whole ship's company to applaud. Even if they thought she ran after young men, and was cheap, they'd applaud. She knew they would!

There was one good thing about the letter, she thought, stepping out of her skirt and leaving it in a ring on the floor: it told her exactly where Angus was, and it wasn't Airdrochan Castle after all, but some-where called Glen Brittle. The name sounded familiar but she couldn't place it for a moment. Then sud-denly she remembered – why, it was where they had filmed the climbing scenes in her film *Pride o' the North*. She'd never been there, of course, since she hadn't been in the climbing sequences – that was the phony part of film-making – but she had seen it when she had attended the film première. She'd have to find out exactly where it was, and how you got there. It was obvious now that Angus couldn't possibly get a letter from her before she arrived herself, as they reached Portree the day after tomorrow and mail took days and days in those out-of-the-world places to get to its destination. She wondered if he and Jaimie were camping out in a tent, or staying at the youth hostel, and if she could stay there too. Oh, well – she'd find out when she got there.

She replaced her mother's letter in its envelope and put it back in the pocket of her skirt. It never occurred to her to put the skirt on a hanger, but she did go so far as to pick it up off the floor and put it over the back of a chair. After this, she looked round for her tights. They ought to be dry by now, she'd washed them through early this morning and hung them in the porthole as usual. But even if they weren't it didn't really matter – they'd cling all the better. Then she gave a gasp of horror . . . where were her tights? The bit of string she had used as a clothes-line was still there, but her tights had disappeared.

The chief engineer, waiting patiently at the end of the corridor for Annette to appear – rather like a cat at a mousehole – heard the sounds of her distress. Being part French, she did nothing by halves – especially anything to do with her emotions. She began to cry, and to stamp her feet. At that moment Gilda Aken-side appeared and the young man drew back into a doorway where he could not be seen. He didn't like Miss Akenside and he certainly didn't want to have to talk to her at this moment. He wanted to talk to Annette, and he intended to talk to Annette if he had to wait here all night. Meanwhile he listened – in fact, he couldn't help hearing – the two of them talking.

'Oh, Gilda!' wailed Annette. 'My tights!'

'What about them?' asked Gilda off-handedly.

'They must have come unpegged,' Annette cried frantically, 'and gone floating out to sea.'

'Just too bad!' drawled Gilda. 'You'll have to dance without them, that's all.'

'But I *can't* dance without them,' said Annette passionately. 'No ballerina dances a classical solo without tights. It just isn't done!'

'Well, one would hardly call you a ballerina, dar-ling, would one?' said Gilda nastily.

Annette was too agitated to snap out the obvious

reply: 'I was billed as a ballerina, anyway, in my film.' She stood in the middle of the cabin, wringing her hands and weeping.

The chief engineer suddenly decided to appear after all, and see if he could help. For the moment he even forgot his quarrel, if you could call it that, with Annette. He strode up to the door and tapped on it, though it was wide open.

'Can I do anything? What's this about tights? You say they have come adrift?'

'Oh, yes,' said Annette, hastily putting on her dressing-gown. She, too, had quite forgotten what had been said about her and the chief engineer. 'I pegged them out on my line – I mean my string – quite carefully. I thought they would dry in the breeze.'

'You pegged them? With what?' demanded the young man.

'With pegs, of course,' snapped Annette. She was far too miserable to be polite. It took a very small thing to make Annette miserable, just as it took a very small thing to make her spirits soar. 'Clothes-pegs.'

'I see,' said the chief engineer. 'Then I take it you imagine the tights floated out of the porthole, leaving the pegs on the line?' He was staring at the string thoughtfully. 'Strange. The pegs don't seem to be here.'

'No, they aren't,' said Annette.

'Well, that's funny,' mused Hamish MacPhee.

'Very funny, if I may say so. One would almost think – ' He was looking straight at Gilda Akenside.

'Almost think what?' said Gilda. 'You aren't suggesting, I hope, that I – '

'I wasn't suggesting anything, my dear,' said the chief engineer. 'I was just wondering.'

'I don't know what you're both talking about,' broke in Annette. 'My tights have gone floating out to sea, and all you can both do is to talk riddles! How can I dance without my tights? I can't dance at all!'

At this dramatic moment the door opened and Janet appeared.

'Oh, Annette, I've been looking everywhere for you. Are these yours? I think they must be.' She held out a long pink object – the missing tights!

'Oh, Janet, where *did* you find them?' exclaimed Annette, hardly able to believe her eyes. 'Wherever were they?'

'Sticking in Linda Boston's porthole,' said Janet, 'and Linda thinks they must have somehow blown out of your cabin, and then been blown into her porthole, because of the way the ship was going, if you see what I mean. Her cabin is nearer the stern.'

The chief engineer was still staring at Gilda Akenside, whose face had fallen.

'I'm still wondering,' he said cryptically as he walked out.

And so Annette, in immaculately fitting, newly washed tights, danced the solo from *The Little Mermaid* in Paddy's evening dress, trimmed with fresh seaweed fished up from Tobermory Bay by Freddie, the bo'sun, and after that, the solo from *The Little Matchgirl*, the ballet that Monsieur Georges had choreographed especially for her. For this dance she wore a piece of sacking made into a ragged dress. To end her performance, she gave them her famous solo from *La Sylphide* out of the film *Pride o' the North*. She had persuaded a shy young man, Michael Dennis by name, to be James, and lie in a chair fast asleep, while she, La Sylphide, the Spirit of the Scottish Woodlands, danced round him. She had made a kilt for Michael out of a tartan rug, and as long as he didn't move it looked quite convincing. She had intended originally to persuade the chief engineer to be James, and then he could have wakened up and danced with her, just like James in the real ballet, but she had pushed the idea firmly out of her mind. She was having nothing more to do with that young man!

But Annette reckoned without his pertinacity and obstinacy. The chief engineer was still waiting for his chance to have it out with her. All during the performance he stood at the back and glowered – as much as a red-haired blue-eyed Scot of his cheerful temperament *could* glower. At the end he strode purposefully and, grasping Annette firmly by one wrist, walked over with her to the microphone that had been installed on deck for the occasion.

'After a short interval,' he announced, 'to allow Miss Dancy to change her costume, she will give you her version of a Highland fling . . . And I shall dance it with you,' he added into Annette's ear.

'No!' said Annette firmly.

'Yes!' said the chief engineer even more firmly. 'Come, below with you! I take it you have a kilt – I have seen you wearing it.'

'It's Janet's,' said Annette. 'I borrowed it.'

'Well, you can borrow it again,' said Hamish Mac-Phee. He himself, being off duty, was wearing full Highland dress – kilt, cut-away jacket, lace at sleeves and neck – the lot! He even had a *sgian dubh* thrust into his tartan stocking. Annette had to admit that he looked magnificent.

He ran her down to the lounge, through the dining-room, along the corridor to her cabin – all without letting go of her wrist. When they arrived at the door he released her.

'Before you change, Annette Dancy,' he said, 'I am wanting to talk to you.'

'Here?' said Annette, her dark eyes wide. It seemed to her a strange place in which to stand talking, this narrow corridor, noisy with the whine of the dynamos and the air-conditioning plant.

'*Here*,' insisted the chief engineer. 'It is against the rules for members of the crew to visit the cabins of passengers, except in emergencies, and as you insist upon avoiding me, I prefer to talk to you here and now. I want to know, and I intend to know, Annette Dancy, what I have done to offend you?'

'Oh, but you haven't done anything,' said Annette.

'Then why are you avoiding me?'

She was silent. She couldn't say she wasn't avoiding him, because it wouldn't be the truth, and anyway it was all too obvious. The corridor tilted gently as the ship lifted and strained at her moorings, and Annette staggered. The chief engineer put out his hand in an involuntary gesture to steady her, then drew it back.

'Well?'

'I'd – I'd rather not say.'

'I see. There is someone else behind all this?'

Annette nodded. She couldn't possibly blurt out, 'Gilda said I was running after you; that the whole ship was laughing at us; that I was making myself cheap.' It would sound too awful! Besides, it would be tale-telling. Gilda had told Annette for her own good – she'd said so.

'I'd rather not talk about it,' she said in her most dignified manner. 'And if you don't mind, I'd rather you didn't talk to me on deck or – or anywhere . . .' Her voice tailed off lamely. It sounded frightful, said that way, but she couldn't help it, since he insisted.

'I see,' said the chief engineer, which was, indeed, far from the truth. Had someone told him that Annette was afraid of people thinking she was running after him, he would certainly have hooted with laughter. Why, he'd spent the entire last two days running after her – literally! Trying vainly to get near enough to her to speak to her.

'I see,' he repeated. 'Well, if that's the way you want it it's certainly okay with me. A very good night to you, Miss Dancy!' The chief engineer had his dignity too!

And so Annette danced the Highland fling by herself after all. While she did it Hamish MacPhee sat locked in his cabin studying a report on light metals in an engineering magazine and trying vainly not to hear the sounds of revelry on the deck. But try as he would, the stirring sounds filtered in through the firmly shut door. He flung the magazine across the little room, stood up and ran his hands through his red hair until it stood on end. Dash it all! He'd liked the little girl! His heart was heavy with anger and disappointment.

As for Annette, she was sad too. If it hadn't been

for Gilda's words, she'd have walked and talked with young Hamish MacPhee and thought nothing of it. They'd have met and parted the best of friends. But now, owing to Gilda's interference, she began to think more seriously about the chief engineer. She had arrived at that dangerous stage when she looked for his coming, even though he kept his back studiously towards her, and if he wasn't there she felt an empty feeling in her heart. She was, you see, standing on the brink of her very first love affair. She was nearly seventeen, which is late to fall in love for the first time. Annette herself didn't realise it, of course, but her feeling for Hamish MacPhee was mostly due to the fact that there didn't happen to be any other interesting young men on board the *Flora Mac-Donald*, and after all he *was* a Scot. She'd always had a weakness for Scots! She cried bitterly into her pillow that night when she was quite sure Gilda was asleep. He really was the dearest boy, and she had offended him terribly. She almost felt like running after him in earnest, and letting Gilda and the whole ship say what they liked!

10   LOCH CORUISK

Annette's time on board the *Flora MacDonald* was rapidly coming to an end. They had sailed past the island of Rhum, with its romantic mountains, and Eigg with its queer hooked top, and now they were approaching Skye. That evening there was to be a fancy dress parade. Usually this event was held at the end of the cruise, but the captain had decided that it would be in the middle this time, so that their celebrity, as they insisted upon calling Annette, would be able to judge the costumes. Who more suitable, pronounced the games committee, who arranged the parade, than a member of the theatrical profession? The ship would arrive at Portree that night, and the next day Annette would go ashore – this time for good. It was a sad thought, everyone agreed! Or at least, not *quite* everyone. There was Gilda Akenside, who was overjoyed to see the last of Annette, and the chief engineer who, so he told himself firmly, 'couldn't care less'.

Meanwhile the ship was sailing straight for Loch

Scavaig on the south-west coast of Skye. Here they would anchor during the afternoon, and the ship's launches would take the passengers ashore, close to Loch Coruisk. Then they would return to the ship and would sail slowly up the east coast of Skye.

The passengers had held a meeting and collected a sum of money with which they had bought the biggest box of chocolates the little shop adjoining the purser's office afforded, and this was to be presented to Annette after she had judged the fancy-dress costumes. Gilda Akenside, as might be expected, had held aloof from all this, but she couldn't help hearing the passengers talking about it. Annette was to sit at the captain's table . . . The ship's cook had made a wonderful cake with ice cream inside, and FAREWELL in icing on top . . . All in honour of Annette! Gilda's heart burned with jealousy. Then there was the fancy dress parade itself – the very idea of Annette's judging the costumes filled Gilda with fury. She knew just how it would be – Annette would give first prize to that stupid Monica Foster, who had bought three rolls of crêpe paper at Oban and had spent all her time fashioning it into an inverted bluebell, and was going as 'Bluebell of Scotland', and she would give second prize to Julia Smith who was going as 'The Cat Who Went On Strike For More Labour-Saving Devices'. Julia had collected up all the ship's mouse-traps, and was wearing them round her waist as a belt, together with a necklace made of pieces of cheese. Yes, Gilda felt sure that Annette wouldn't even give her a consolation prize for her beautiful 'Eighteenth-Century Lady' that she had hired in London! The more Gilda thought about it, the more she hated the very idea of Annette's last evening aboard the *Flora MacDonald*. But what could she do about it? Seemingly nothing. But couldn't she? An idea flashed into her brain – an idea that was so brilliant yet so staggeringly simple that it made her gasp. Of course it might not come off, but it was worth trying . . .

Imagine a small dark-blue loch, with scarcely an island to reflect in its surface and no softening vegetation on its stony banks, a loch entirely surrounded by a ring of deeply seamed, wrinkled, craggy grey mountains, rising in great precipitous leaps into the limpid sky. Loch Coruisk and the famous Cuillin Hills of Skye!

There is no road leading to this remote stretch of dark water. To reach it by land you must scramble many rough miles down Glen Sligachan, and even when you finally reach the Druim Hain Ridge, from where you can look down upon the loch, you have still a long and weary climb down the scree to its desolate shores three hundred metres below. Annette's old gentleman had shown it all to her on his Ordnance Survey sheet, pointing the route out with his silver pencil.

'Oh, do you mind if I borrow your map for a

minute?' she had said. 'I want to find out where Glen Brittle is, and how I'm to get there when we reach Portree.'

He had handed over the map and lent her his pencil, and she had made a rough sketch on the back of her mother's letter that she had pulled out of her pocket.

'We're here now – ' pointing with the pencil ' – just sailing into Loch Scavaig. And *there's* Glen Brittle! It looks awfully near – as if you could climb straight over to it from Coruisk.'

'I hope you aren't thinking of doing anything like that,' the old gentleman had said anxiously. He seemed to be very knowledgeable about mountains. 'You would have the main Cuillin range to negotiate, and none of the passes is much lower than three thousand feet! Far, far too tough for a young lady like you. A better way would be from the far side of the loch up on to the Druim Hain Ridge. Then – ' pointing to it ' – down the other side, and along Glen Sligachan to the hotel at the foot, where you could get a bus down to Glen Brittle. The path from the Druim Hain Ridge takes you past these two tiny lochans. They're called the Dubh Lochs because they are black, and this fine mountain towering over them is called Blaven.'

'I know! I know!' Annette had cried excitedly. 'I've climbed it.'

The old gentleman had looked at her with respect, and more than a little astonishment. He'd certainly never thought of a fairylike ballet dancer like Annette climbing mountains, even an easy one like Blaven.

'Well, well!' he had said. 'All the same, the main Cuillin range is a tough proposition – far too tough for a child like you.'

'Then it's a good thing I'm going to Portree in the *Flora MacDonald* tonight, isn't it,' Annette had laughed, 'or I might be tempted!'

Annette was in the last boat ashore. She had been so busy ironing her ballet-dress in readiness for tonight's festivities that she'd almost missed the launch as usual! There were only one or two people in the boat, since most of them had gone ashore earlier. Gilda Akenside was one of them and, strangely enough, she was exceedingly friendly and had insisted upon accompanying Annette quite a long way along the Coruisk shore. Most of the other passengers were either sunning themselves on the warm rocks or taking photographs, making the most of the wonderful weather. They might never again, as the purser had pointed out that morning, see the celebrated Loch Coruisk under such perfect conditions. Usually people saw it through a curtain of rain, or shrouded in mist. Often they never saw it at all! Even the crew were standing on deck and exclaiming at the sight, all except the chief engineer who stayed in his cabin and, when he did come out for a breath of fresh air, was careful to keep on the side of the ship where he couldn't see the little launches bobbing up and down on the sunlit blue waters of Scavaig, and Annette Dancy in one of them!

As for Annette, how she wished she had had the young man's company for this expedition of all expeditions. Gilda Akenside was no substitute at all. Annette wanted to know how and when these mountains were formed, and she felt sure that Hamish MacPhee would know – he was that kind of a young man. He was so interesting. He would know what all their names were, and how you pronounced them.

'I think I'll just sit down here,' said Gilda at length, 'and leave you to go on by yourself, Annette.

My feet get so sore on these awful stones!'

Secretly Annette was rather pleased. If she couldn't have the companion of her choice, she would rather be alone.

'All right,' she said. 'I want to walk on as far as the next point, and then perhaps I shall be able to see right into that huge corrie.'

'Don't forget – last launch at five o'clock,' shouted Gilda after her. 'Five o'clock!'

'Five o'clock?' repeated Annette. 'I thought it was four. Well, it's all the better, I shall have two whole hours to explore. I'll be able to walk miles and miles in that time!'

Gilda said nothing to that. The farther Annette walked the better she'd be pleased! Anyway, her companion was nearly out of sight round the nearest spur of rock by this time. She smiled to herself, and stretched in the sun like a cat. Her plan was going to work!

As is usually the case, Annette found that when she reached what she had thought to be the best vantage point for a view into the corrie, there was still a shoulder of mountain in the way. Just a bit farther, and she'd be able to see round the corner. A bit farther, a bit farther! Time crept on, and when she looked at her watch she was amazed to find it was half past three. That was half time, but of course she'd go back faster – one always did! Still, she couldn't go much farther, only just round the next corner. By now she was nearly at the head of the loch. In another ten minutes she had reached it, and then, having taken one long look into Coir-Uisg, she turned her back firmly on the beckoning ridges and began to retrace her steps.

It was half past four when she got within sight of the lower end of the loch. She could not see the waiting boat of course, since it would be actually in Loch Scavaig, drawn up alongside the big rock that acted as a jetty. Strange to say, none of the passengers were sitting about either. Even Gilda had disappeared.

How funny! thought Annette. They must all have gone back in the earlier launches. Evidently the passengers of the *Flora MacDonald* thought more about their tea than the famous Loch Coruisk!

But when she came out into Loch Scavaig, there was no ship's launch waiting at the stone jetty for her. Nor was there a ship. The bay was completely empty, except for a flock of black-headed gulls, rocking up and down on the waves. The *Flora MacDonald* had vanished!

For a long moment Annette stood there, her head whirling. Had she, by chance, come out into the wrong bay? She knew it was fatally easy to do such things in a mountainous country. But no, she recognised the hills standing sentinel on either side – Sgurr na Stri and Gars Bheinn. She remembered the boatman telling the Slaughters, the Americans who rented Jaimie's castle, their names when they had all visited Loch Coruisk last summer. It was quite obvious to her now that there had been an awful mistake and that the ship had gone without her. She looked down at her wristwatch again so as to make quite certain of the time. Ten minutes to five . . . No, it hadn't stopped. She simply couldn't imagine what had happened!

11   LOST – ONE DANCER!

To say that Annette's disappearance caused a disturbance on board the *Flora MacDonald* is putting it mildly. There in all its glory stood the captain's table, with the special place, marked with a corsage of delicate freesias, for the guest of honour – Annette – at his right hand. The table itself was beautifully decorated with hothouse flowers that had been bought at Oban and kept in the ship's refrigerator for this important occasion. The big doors that divided the dining-room from the card room had been folded back, and extra tables had been brought in, so that all the passengers could dine together and so miss none of the fun!

And now everyone was assembled – some in fancy dress, others in evening-dress. Only one passenger was missing, and that was the person it was all in honour of – Annette herself! The captain smiled indulgently. He supposed the little girl was finishing off her ballet-dress or something of the sort. He said grace, and they all sat down and began to talk to pass away the time. She would come, surely, in a minute or two. But the minutes passed and still no Annette. A steward was sent to her cabin, only to return with the news that she was not there.

'Miss Akenside,' said the Captain, walking across to Annette's usual table, 'Miss Dancy shares a cabin with you, I believe. Have you any idea where she is?'

Gilda coloured and began to stammer.

'No – yes – I really don't know.'

'Come, my dear young lady, you must know whether she was there or not when you dressed for dinner?' said the captain tartly. He disliked Gilda Akenside exceedingly, although she had sailed in his ship probably more than anyone else. 'She did dress for dinner, I suppose?'

'No,' said Gilda, 'she didn't.'

'Not dress?' echoed the captain. 'You mean she didn't actually put on her dress, or do you mean she was not there to put it on?'

'She wasn't there,' said Gilda. 'At least, I didn't see her.'

A hum of excited conversation buzzed round the room. Everyone began to talk at once. The captain tapped on the table for silence.

'You say you think she wasn't there?' persisted the captain, turning back to Gilda. '*Why* wasn't she there? When did you last see her?'

'At – Loch Coruisk,' said Gilda truthfully.

'Didn't she come back with you?'

'No – not in my boat.'

The two sailors who had comprised the boat's crew were sent for. No, Miss Dancy wasn't in the last launch, they assured the captain. They'd asked about her most particularly, and the young lady, indicating Gilda, had told them she'd gone back to the ship in an earlier launch.

'Well, I thought she had,' said Gilda sulkily. 'Unless it was someone else I saw – someone very like her. Anyway, it was four o'clock. She ought to have been there.'

'That is quite beside the point,' snapped the captain. 'The point is, it looks very much as if the poor child has been left at Loch Coruisk.' The affectionate way in which he referred to Annette as 'the poor child' annoyed Gilda still more. But what Gilda didn't realise, or what she didn't care to realise, was that there are no buses at Loch Coruisk and the nearest village is many miles away, and well nigh inaccessable into the bargain.

The captain had risen from the table and left the room abruptly, leaving things in charge of the purser, and a dismal meal it was. No one was sure, you see, what had really happened to Annette. It certainly looked as if she had been accidentally left at Coruisk, but there was always the possibility that something even worse had befallen her. One helpful lady vowed she had seen Annette dressed for dinner leaning over the rail on the boat deck. Suppose she had fallen over . . .

'Nonsense!' snapped the purser. 'No one could fall over the rail in calm weather. It's a sheer impossibility.' All the same, the passengers couldn't help wondering. Someone else came forward and said she had sat at the next table to Annette at teatime. Oh, yes, of course she was sure it was Annette. You couldn't mistake her, could you – not even a back view? The purser didn't reply as he would have liked to: 'You could, my dear lady!'

Yes, there were all sorts of rumours, but the bulk of the passengers were quite sure that Annette had forgotten the time and was now languishing on the shores of Loch Coruisk.

'Imagine it, my dear,' said a Miss MacNaughton, who sat at Annette's table, to Miss Hepple, 'left all by herself on the shores of that god-forsaken lake, poor little thing! Why, they say it's haunted by one of those water-horses that the Skye folk believe in. Some people say it's a huge monster like the one in Loch Ness, and I must say I wouldn't be surprised at its being haunted by anything, would you? Quite awe-inspiring enough in the sunlight and with other people around, but think of it at night with all those glowering mountains and a mist coming up. Not a house for miles and miles! No way of getting to anywhere except up those dreadful screes or whatever they call them, or, of course, by boat. One could easily wander about for days and die of exhaustion without anyone knowing . . . '

Gilda, listening to all this, began to grow really frightened. She wished with all her heart she hadn't done what she had, not because of any kind feeling for Annette, but for fear of what the consequences to herself would be if anything happened to her.

And now Mr Blount, Annette's old gentleman, added to her fears:

'The last time I saw the little girl was just before we dropped anchor in Scavaig,' he said. 'She asked to see my map, and we talked about the various ways of getting to places in Skye. She wanted to know where Glen Brittle was, and I showed her. She said that it looked as if you could easily get over to Glen Brittle from the shores of Coruisk. I assured her that it is not so – that one would have to cross the main Cuillin range. You don't suppose – '

'No, I do *not*!' exclaimed the chief engineer, breaking rudely into the conversation. He was shocked out of his usual polite manner by the terrible fear that the old gentleman might be right. It was just the sort of hare-brained thing Annette would do in her impetuous headlong way – leave the ship at Coruisk and try to climb over to Glen Brittle from there! Then he rejected the theory. It didn't make sense. If Annette had been going to do that, she'd have said so. She would have told the captain anyway, since she knew full well he was holding a special dinner-party in her honour. Besides, she was judging the fancy dress costumes . . . No, in spite of all the people who had seen and spoken to her, or said they had, he was quite sure in his own mind that she had been left behind at Coruisk. Perhaps she had been dreaming about her ballet and had forgotten the time. Or perhaps her watch had stopped. Or perhaps she had fallen and sprained – or broken – her ankle. A hundred things might have happened to her . . . He determined that as soon as they reached Kyleakin he would be in the first boat to go back and look for her. In the stress of the moment all his anger against her was forgotten.

Meanwhile Annette, having made sure that she *was* in the right bay, and that the boat and the ship had really gone away without her, sat down on the edge of the loch to collect her thoughts. It wouldn't be long before they missed her, she thought. When she didn't turn up in her cabin to dress for dinner, Gilda would remember that she had, mistakenly, told her the last boat left at five o'clock. Surely they would come back for her? It wasn't as if she had done it deliberately, or even thoughtlessly. If anybody was to blame, it was Gilda. Never, even in her wildest imaginings, did Annette guess the truth – that Gilda had done it on purpose, and would therefore be the very last person to give the alarm.

When seven o'clock came and still no sign of a rescue boat, Annette began to think that they were not coming back for her. She remembered a notice that adorned the board outside the purser's office:

PASSENGERS WHO DO NOT ARRIVE AT THE LAUNCHES AT THE TIMES SPECIFIED RUN THE RISK OF BEING LEFT BEHIND, AS THE SHIP OBVIOUSLY CANNOT WAIT FOR STRAGGLERS.

She took her mother's letter out of her pocket and studied the sketch-map on the back. Never had she expected to be using it in such dramatic circumstances! Here was Loch Coruisk, and here was she! There was literally nowhere for her to go unless she climbed up the side of the loch on to the Druim Hain Ridge, as pointed out by her old gentleman, and make her way to Sligachan at the foot of the glen of that name. She remembered passing the hotel in the Slaughters' car on their way from the Skye Gathering Ball at Portree. It looked a friendly place. She was sure when she got there they would help her to get to Glen Brittle where Jaimie and Angus were.

She got up from the stone which was growing chilly. She had made up her mind – she would go to Sligachan.

She began to walk round the foot of the loch until she came to the river flowing out of Coruisk. It was quite swift and deep, and she had to wade through it, carrying her shoes. At the head of the loch the inviting corrie didn't look inviting any more. It was

filled with mist and the shadows of evening. She walked on as quickly as she could, up and down, squelching through boggy ground, sometimes at the water's edge and sometimes high above the loch, until she struck a footpath gradually ascending away from the shore, in the direction of a waterfall some way ahead. It was eight o'clock when she got there, and the sun was setting. Moreover the mist was spreading, and was already forming in thick banks over the precipitous slopes of the mountains, hiding their razor-sharp spires and pinnacles.

She sat down for a few minutes to rest by the stream, and while she sat there it seemed to her that the peaks lifted their jagged heads out of the mist, one by one, and solemnly said 'Goodnight' to her. Then quietly they withdrew behind their white curtains.

'Oh, but it's not goodnight!' Annette cried aloud to them. 'I have a lot more climbing to do before I can say that!' She rose and began to scramble up towards the lochan she knew she must pass to reach the Druim Hain Ridge. After about an hour's climbing she reached the cloud bank and had to stop to put on her mackintosh, which until now she had carried strapped to her back, rucksack fashion. It was lucky she had brought it, she thought – she'd been in two minds whether to do so or not. Her fingers, feeling in the pockets, found a block of chocolate and a few biscuits. She ate a little of the former and a couple of biscuits and plodded on. She couldn't help thinking of that other time when she had been lost in the mist of the Isle of Arran – she and the chief engineer. She wondered what he had said when he found she was missing. And then there was the dinner party. She didn't know, of course, about all the things that were being done in her honour, but she knew she was supposed to be sitting at the captain's table and judging the fancy dress afterwards. Who would judge them now? Gilda, perhaps. At this very moment they would just be finishing dinner . . .

So preoccupied was she with her own thoughts that she didn't notice for quite a long time that she had climbed right up through the cloud bank into the bright moonlight on the other side. She had got to the top of the first part of the steep slope, and had reached a kind of plateau. Over to her left was a small lochan, fed by a brawling stream which entered at one end in a series of miniature waterfalls and rushed out at the other in its headlong descent to Coruisk. She remembered the old gentleman pointing it out, so at least she knew she was on the right track.

She stopped for a moment and looked round her, awestricken at the sight of this great mountain range, its height increased by the mist, standing out, jagged as a saw, against the clear sky. Suddenly she was frightened – more frightened than she had ever been in her life. There was something alive and terrible about these stone giants. They stood there in a ring round her, regarding her menacingly. If she lost her way, or made one false step, they would fling her down a precipice, and then, when winter came, they would cover her up with snow, and no one would ever know what had become of Annette Dancy. She wanted to fling herself down on the ground, to cover her face with her hands and shut out the awful sight, to scream in terror, but a lump rose in her throat, choking her. Then she pulled herself together. It wouldn't help to become hysterical, and after all they were only mountains, and – one must admit – they were beautiful, even if they were awe-inspiring. That one, with a floating cloud of mist about it, looked just like a fairy castle sticking up out of the sea at the end of a rocky causeway. Then, as she stood there, she heard, far, far below her, a thin whistle. There were lights too appearing and disappearing out of the mist. She knew what it was – a boat had at last been sent to pick her up!

Now what was she to do? It had taken her more than two hours to climb up here. How long would it take her to climb down again? An experienced mountaineer might do it in a short time, she supposed, but she knew it would take her hours. Although up here everything was almost as bright as day, down there in the mist it would be quite dark. She'd probably lose her way, or fall over a precipice, and almost certainly by the time she got down to the lochside, if she ever did get down, the boat would have gone, and all her trouble would have been for nothing. She tried shouting, and although her voice was echoed again and again by the great mountain walls, she guessed that it would be muffled by the bank of mist that

rolled between her and the loch, three hundred
metres below, and would never reach the searchers.
  And sure enough, after about half an hour, the
lights disappeared and the whistle ceased to sound.

The chief engineer, for it was he, had decided that Annette was certainly not on the shores of Coruisk, which, of course, was right, and, with a heavy heart, he climbed back into the motor-launch and chugged out of Loch Scavaig back to Portree to report his failure to the captain.

Annette climbed on past the lochan to the top of the ridge where the ground was drier. She chose a flat piece of ground, sheltered by an overhanging rock, removed some of the sharpest of the stones, wrapped herself up in her mackintosh, and went to sleep. Fortunately the weather remained dry, and she woke in the very early morning, stiff and tired and bitterly cold but otherwise none the worse for her adventure. She ate the rest of the chocolate and the biscuits, washing them down with a drink of ice-cold water out of a nearby stream, then took another look at her mother's letter. Yes, it was obvious she was on top of the Druim Hain Ridge. Now all she had to do was to turn her back on Coruisk and find the path down to the two little lochans that her old gentleman had pointed out, and which lay in Glen Sligachan. They were near the foot of Blaven, so oughtn't to be hard to find. She climbed up to a viewpoint and looked round, and sure enough she could see the rocky top of Blaven.

Soon she was in Glen Sligachan, and there were the *dubh* lochans – living up to their name! Two blacker or more sinister stretches of water Annette thought she had never seen.

125

Annette plodded on, soaked to the skin, footsore but undaunted. Thank goodness she was wearing walking shoes, which, although they squelched at every step, protected her feet, for the going was rough in the extreme. In fact it was so rough, and Annette was picking her way so carefully round half-hidden rocks, streams, tussocks of rough grass and rushes, not to mention patches of treacherous boggy ground, green as emerald, that she didn't see the two young men until she was almost up to them, and, for the same reason, they didn't see her. Then they all stopped short in amazement.

'Annette!' exclaimed Angus MacCrimmon. 'How

in the name of wonder did you get up here?'

And 'Angus!' cried Annette. 'Oh, how nice to see you, and Jaimie too. How did you know I was here? I climbed up the mountain side from that lake – you know the one? Its name is Loch Coruisk.'

'I am knowing its name well enough,' said Angus with a faint smile. His face was drawn and haggard with anxiety. 'Nothing have I heard in this island during the last twelve hours but Loch Coruisk and the little girl, Annette Dancy, marooned and perhaps lost on its shores. And now, just when Jaimie and I are coming down to rescue you, we find you up here in Glen Sligachan!'

'Well, what was I to do?' demanded Annette. 'I couldn't stay down there for ever! I'd have died of hunger.'

'We naturally thought, Jaimie and I, that you would remain where you were until help came,' said Angus. 'That would have been the sensible thing to do. But then you never were sensible, were you, Annette?' Now that his anxiety was over he had a mind to scold her. She ought to have had more sense than to go wandering about in the Cuillins all by herself!

'I *did* stay where I was,' Annette told him. 'I sat there for hours and hours – well, two, anyway – but nobody came, so I thought I would help myself. Personally I think I had a lot of sense. Anyway, I'm quite all right, so why all the fuss?'

'Only that the whole island is out searching for

you,' said Angus. 'We must get back to the Sligachan Hotel as quickly as possible and let them know that you are found. The *Flora MacDonald* lies anchored in Portree Bay, and the captain and crew and all the passengers are frantic with anxiety.'

'Oh, I'm *so* sorry,' exclaimed Annette. 'But really it wasn't my fault. You see, Gilda – she's one of my cabin-mates – well, she told me that the last launch left Coruisk at five o'clock, but it must have left earlier, so – '

'We will hear all about it as we walk,' said Angus, turning back along the track to Sligachan. 'Come along with you now!'

Jaimie, as usual, had said nothing. A more silent man than Jaimie Gordon Annette thought she had never met. And then, as they walked back along the glen in single file, Annette between the two men, he suddenly asked, 'What was it you were saying, Annette, about someone telling you wrongly about the time of the boat?'

'Yes, it was Gilda,' answered Annette. '*I* thought the boatman said the last launch left at four o'clock, and Gilda and I walked along the shore, and I wanted to go a bit farther by myself, because her feet hurt, and she shouted after me, "Don't forget – the last launch is at five." I'm sure she said five, because I asked her again, and she repeated it. She must have been mistaken.'

'I see,' said Jaimie. 'But Gilda, I gather, did *not* miss the launch?'

'No, she didn't,' said Annette. 'She went back in an earlier one, which was awfully lucky, wasn't it?'

'It was indeed,' agreed Jaimie. 'I am wondering if, perhaps, this Gilda wished you to miss the boat for some reason?'

'Oh, *no!*' said Annette, shocked. 'Why should Gilda have wanted to do that?'

'I do not know,' said Jaimie quietly, 'but I have known some girls who would do such a thing – for jealousy, perhaps.'

'But why should anyone – least of all Gilda – be jealous of me?' asked Annette, a pucker between her eyebrows. 'Gilda is so pretty, and I'm as plain as a pikestaff.'

Angus, looking back at her as she ploughed manfully through the wet heather, didn't agree. He thought Annette was beautiful wherever she was, or whatever she was wearing, and now, with the raindrops clinging to her eyelashes and falling off the end of her nose, he thought she was entrancing.

'Oh, I expect it was just me, really,' said Annette humbly. 'As Angus says, I always was scatterbrained! And by the way, Jaimie, I do hope you got my letter, and that you don't mind my coming to stay with you at Airdrochan Castle? Oh, but I forgot, you aren't at Airdrochan just now – you're in a tent or somewhere down at Glen Brittle. Well, perhaps I could stay at the youth hostel.'

'I am getting your letter, Annette,' answered Jaimie in his old-fashioned, polite way, 'and I am, of course, most honoured for you to pay me a visit. Angus and I have finished our work down at Glen Brittle, so we should have been returning to Airdrochan anyhow. I have persuaded Mary Gordon to bring Sheena from Glendounie to stay with us too, so that you will not be without a chaperone.'

'Oh, Jaimie, you dear, funny, Highland man!' exclaimed Annette. 'Fancy thinking of a chaperone for me! I thought chaperones were as dead as the dodo!'

'You will not find Mary Gordon as dead as the dodo, I assure you!' laughed Jaimie in his turn. 'She is very much alive, indeed.'

'And Sheena? Is Sheena well?' asked Annette. She had no great liking for Angus's cousin, but thought it polite to ask about her, since she was also Jaimie's ward.

'Sheena is very well, thank you,' answered Jaimie, and nothing in his tone betrayed what he felt for his beautiful ward. 'As you no doubt know, Sheena's home, Glendounie House, has been turned into a hotel. Mrs Gordon manages the financial side, and Sheena acts as hostess.'

'Oh, she'll be wonderful at that!' cried Annette. 'She's so beautiful, people will come just to see her.'

'That is possible,' said Jaimie drily. Only too possible, he thought – especially young men! He had not visualised that when he put the proposition to his young ward that she might run a guest-house. He had merely thought it would amuse her until she was old enough to marry. As to whether he would marry her himself, he had not yet decided. He knew quite certainly, however, that he did not wish, nor intend, her to marry anybody else. Annette, looking at his handsome face with its brooding, dark eyes, wondered what he was thinking. She would have been surprised had she known!

After a time the extreme roughness of the path began to tell upon Annette, and she began to stumble over the hidden boulders and tufts of long grass. After all, she had had an exhausting time during the last twenty-four hours, and only sheer determination and nervous energy had kept her going. The two young men clasped hands and made a seat for her, and so, with an arm about the neck of each, they came at last to Sligachan, where the lonely hotel stands all by itself at the crossroads.

They were welcomed by the owner himself, Ian Campbell, and by the guests, all of whom had heard, it seemed, about the little dancer who had been marooned down on the shores of lonely Loch Coruisk. When they learned that she had climbed up on the Druim Hain Ridge, and had spent the night there, they were appalled. Hadn't she been scared to death?

'Why, no!' laughed Annette. 'At least, only for a minute. Then I thought – what should I be scared of? They're only mountains, and there was a moon and a lot of stars. I was pretty hungry though!' She was in the dining-room by this time having a wonderful meal, while Angus and Jaimie rang up the shipping office at Portree to let the captain of the *Flora MacDonald* know that Annette had been found and was safe, and that the ship could proceed on her way.

They came back in a few minutes to say that the captain sent his love to Annette – yes, in spite of all the trouble and anxiety she had caused – and reminded her that the *Flora MacDonald* would anchor in Broadford Bay on her return journey from Stornaway in the Outer Isles, and that a launch would be sent ashore for their little dancer and they would have their dinner-party after all. Yes, and she should judge the fancy dress parade as well. It was the express wish of all the passengers. Oh, and she could bring her friends aboard too, if she cared. And there was the question of her clothes – the captain would see that they were packed up and sent over to the shipping office before the ship left Portree. She could collect them there.

'Oh, the dear, darling man!' exclaimed Annette, when she heard all this. Then, to everyone's consternation she burst into tears. 'I – I'm so h-happy!' she sobbed.

12 THE ISLE OF SKYE

Airdrochan Castle hadn't changed a bit, thought Annette. Although Jaimie had done a good deal for his village with the money he had made with his one film, *Pride o' the North*, he hadn't spent a penny on the castle itself – at least, not so that you'd notice. It now had electric power instead of oil lamps and candles, it is true, and the rough causeway connecting the ancient building with the mainland had been mended in places, but that was the sum total of the improvements.

As far as the little village, or *clachan*, as it was called, was concerned, it was quite another matter. The cottages had been badly in need of repairs. Some of them had had holes in the roofs, and walls too, and others were so dark and damp inside that they were quite unfit to live in. There were even one or two 'black' houses, made of stacked peat, with open hearths and holes in the roof to let the smoke out! The villagers hadn't complained. They had known that the laird, or 'Himself' as they usually referred to him, could do nothing about it. He was as poor as they, in spite of his castle. But now, since the making of the film, everything was different. The 'black' houses had been turned into sheds for storing hay, new cottages had been built and new byres for the cattle. The whole village had been wired for electricity, and now it winked and twinkled cheerfully on the eastern shore of Loch Slapin.

Annette, as she went round the village visiting the people she had met and made friends with during her last visit, noticed all these things, and came to the conclusion that Jaimie, in spite of the strange ruthless streak that was in him, was really an exceedingly nice man and, moreover, an uncommonly good landlord.

It was a pity, she thought, that more of the poverty-stricken Scottish lairds couldn't be given film contracts, so that they could do what Jaimie Gordon had done!

And so her short week at Airdrochan Castle passed away, as quickly as holidays do when you are enjoying every minute of them. She received a letter from her mother, written from Kandersteg in Switzerland. It had been sent on from the convent home by the faithful Paddy, and so was nearly a week late. Mr and Mrs MacCrimmon – Annette had to think hard for a moment to realise that this was her mother! – were having a wonderful time, it seemed.

'Angus,' she said, folding up the letter and putting it back in her pocket, 'have you ever been to Switzerland?'

'Yes,' said Angus, tossing a stone down into the Shoot, and listening to the echo it made as it ricocheted from side to side. 'I went there with my father three years ago – that was just before I met you, Annette.' Angus dated every event from the time he met Annette. 'We climbed several peaks in the Valais, and also in the Bernese Oberland.'

'And did you love it?' she asked wistfully.

'Well enough,' answered Angus gravely. 'It was very beautiful, but not at all like this.' His eyes wandered round the vast lonely corries, the splintered peaks, the black glistening rock faces, with the grey scree-slopes in between. 'These mountains are more like the Austrian Dolomites. Yes, I love the Cuillins even more than the Alps, but this may well be because I was born and bred here in Skye. The Cuillin Hills are *my* mountains! Every Skye man feels so, and that is why, if Skye people leave their homes, they never forget the island of their birth, even if they can never come back there to live.'

Suddenly a cold breath stole over them. The sun had gone in and a cloud of mist boiled up at their feet, swirling round the jagged peaks, and finally blotting them out altogether.

'Ugh!' said Annette with a shiver. 'How cold it is! Hadn't we better go down. I had no idea the weather was going to change so suddenly.'

'Wait you!' said Angus and, taking a sweater out of his rucksack, he folded it round her shoulders. Together they sat there, enveloped in the grey wet cloud, two solitary figures in a dead white world. And then, just as if invisible fingers had parted the misty curtain, a hole appeared, and down below Coire Lagan appeared. The sun was shining on the flat grey rocks, and turning the tiny lochan lying on the floor of the corrie to a shining golden coin. Then, as suddenly as it had appeared, the mist rolled away and vanished completely and the air was suddenly hot and blue again.

'How strange!' said Annette, throwing off Angus's sweater. 'Where has it gone to? The mist, I mean.'

Angus laughed.

'That is one of the secrets of the Cuillin of Skye,' he said. 'No one knows!'

'What a pity we can't see Loch Scavaig from here,' Annette said after a while. 'The *Flora MacDonald* was due there this afternoon, and this evening she anchors in Broadford Bay. I'm getting terribly excited about the dinner-party tonight. Oughtn't we to be going down now?'

'It will not take long,' Angus assured her. 'A six hundred metre scree-slope is a wearisome thing to climb up, but one can descend very quickly – in fact, in a matter of minutes.'

'You might,' said Annette, 'but not me. I daren't skate down scree-slopes because of my precious ankles. My living is in my feet, you know!'

They moved round their rocky perch a little, in order to follow the sun.

'It doesn't seem like a whole week since I climbed up from Coruisk and met you and Jaimie in Glen Sligachan, does it?' said Annette, sitting down again, this time with her legs dangling over a hundred-and-fifty metre drop. 'It's dreadful to think that I shall be going back to London the day after tomorrow. You see, I must be back there on Sunday night. So I must set off on Saturday morning at the latest, because it takes more than a day to get to London. If only the *Flora MacDonald* sailed a bit faster I could have travelled back in her, but she takes a week, and doesn't dock at Liverpool until midday Thursday, which is far too late for me. It's a shame though, because I hate travelling by train all by myself – it's so awfully dull!'

Angus was silent.

'Poor Sheena,' said Annette after a while. 'Fancy having to miss this wonderful climb just to go over the accounts of Glendounie House with Jaimie! I do think he might have done it some other time.'

'I do not think that Sheena will be minding going over the accounts with Jaimie,' observed Angus enigmatically, 'nor that Jaimie will mind it either. By the way, Annette, did your mother – our mother – say in her letter when she and my father would be returning to England?'

'Oh, yes,' answered Annette. 'Didn't I tell you? They're coming back to London on Monday. That's another reason why I must leave here on Saturday. She says we're all going to celebrate.' Her face grew suddenly grave. 'Angus,' she went on, 'I've been wanting to ask you something – in fact, that was really partly why I wanted so much to come to Skye, so that we could talk about it. What did you think about your father and my mother getting married? Weren't you rather shaken? I mean, didn't you think they were rather old to get married again? After all, there was Daddy – '

'I have thought about it a very great deal,' Angus told her, 'and the more I have thought, the more it seems to me that they were right to do it. My father was all alone, except for me, and I am grown up now, and your mother – '

'She had *me*!' broke in Annette.

'Had she?' asked Angus gravely. 'I had an idea that

you, Annette, had gone dancing away to London to make your own life.'

'But I wrote to her,' said Annette, 'and I rang her up every Sunday.'

'Of course,' said Angus, 'but you led your own life all the same, and quite right too. It would have been very wrong indeed of you not to have done so, now that you are grown up. The question is – are you really grown up, Annette, or are you still – still . . . ' He hesitated, trying to find words to make his meaning clear. '. . . Still standing on the threshold of life, as it were?'

'You mean in the wings,' said Annette, putting it into theatrical language as usual. 'I know that's how it is with my dancing! I'm always watching someone else dance the principal role, and never doing it myself. But I don't think it's fair to say, Angus, that I'm not grown up. I'm seventeen – almost. Seventeen is quite grown up.'

'It is not a question of age,' stated Angus. 'Some people who are seventy years old are not yet grown up.'

'You're talking in riddles!' declared Annette. 'How could anyone seventy not be grown up?' Then she stood up and stretched herself. 'But now I've asked you, I know how you feel. I'm going down now – there's another cloud coming.'

They descended to the col, and thence down the Stone Shoot. Angus skated on ahead, digging in his heels, and then waiting for Annette to follow more

141

cautiously. The noise of the stones rattling down between the walls of the great dark gully echoed and re-echoed until the chasm was filled with tumultuous sound.

13 THE *FLORA MACDONALD*
AGAIN

That night, the four of them – Sheena, Jaimie, Angus and Annette – stepped into the waiting launch at Broadford, and were taken swiftly out to the *Flora MacDonald*. The little white ship lay out in the bay, ablaze with light from prow to stern, which reflected in the calm waters of the harbour. At the end of their journey they were met by the captain, the purser and the chief engineer, who had forgotten his quarrel with Annette. In the background, wearing her costume of an eighteenth-century lady, was Gilda Akenside. For a few days after the scare about Annette's disappearance, she had walked about looking very subdued. She had been really frightened, though not repentant, at what she had done, but now she had recovered all her former self-assurance. She wasn't feeling at all pleased that the dinner-party was being held tonight after all, not to mention the fancy dress parade.

'Oh, hello, Annette,' she said when they met. 'What a shock you gave us, disappearing like that, and after all the times I told you not to miss the last boat!'

'Are you sure, Miss Akenside, that you told Miss Dancy the right time for the last boat?' said a voice over Annette's shoulder – the lilting Gaelic voice of Jaimie Gordon. There was something in the gentle tones, or perhaps it was the expression in the young Highlander's dark eyes, that made Gilda turn red and begin to stammer. Meanwhile the chief engineer was looking with open curiosity at Annette's friends.

'Oh, Hamish,' she said, 'this is Angus MacCrimmon. Angus, Mr MacPhee.'

'Your brother?' said the chief engineer.

'Sort of,' agreed Annette, while Angus explained: 'My father is quite recently married to Annette's mother, which makes us step-brother and sister.'

'Ah, I see,' said Hamish MacPhee, his face falling. Then this, said his expression, was the reason for Annette's strange behaviour – she had a young man up her sleeve all the time! As for Angus, he noticed the way the chief engineer looked at Annette, and knew that the young man was attracted to her. It was a good thing, thought Angus, that the *Flora MacDonald* was sailing away with the morning tide without Annette! Otherwise there would be one more broken heart. Annette had a habit of breaking men's hearts without even knowing that she had as much as cracked them! She was just a betwixt and between – half child, half woman! She stood in the wings of life, as she herself had said.

*   *   *

144

The dinner was all that it should be. The cook had produced an even bigger cake filled with ice cream, and decorated with FAREWELL in cherries on the top. Although there was no bouquet of hothouse flowers for the guest of honour, someone had gone ashore and picked a nosegay of wild ones that pleased Annette even more. The purser had carefully kept the box of chocolates under the counter of his little shop, and now he produced it, to be presented to Annette later in the evening.

And now came the judging of the fancy dress costumes. Annette gave Monica Fraser as 'Bluebell of Scotland' the first prize, as Gilda had known she

would, and a young man called Derick got second prize as 'The Hunchback of Notre-Dame'. He wore a nylon stocking pulled tightly over his face to give it the misshapen features of the dwarf, and a cushion strapped to his back, underneath his coat, for the hump. The prize for the most original costume went to Julia as 'The Cat Who Went On Strike For More Labour-Saving Devices'. Gilda was told politely but firmly by the purser that the judge and committee felt unable to award her a prize for her costume since it had obviously not been made on board ship.

'It's her fault!' said Gilda to herself, looking angrily across the lounge at Annette, who was by now the centre of a crowd of passengers who were all hearing about their little dancer's night out at Loch Coruisk. 'They'd never have thought of it if she hadn't suggested it.' Which was quite untrue, since, although it had occurred to Annette, the purser had mentioned it first and had himself declared Gilda disqualified.

And then it was time for Annette to dance. She had run down to her old cabin on the main deck and put on her ballet-dress that Angus had carried for her in the boat, together with her make-up and Paddy's evening dress. She was ready in a few minutes, and up she ran again on to the crowded sports deck. She gave them a classical solo out of *Coppelia*, that enchanting ballet about an old toymaker who made with his hands a life-sized doll, which suddenly became alive and behaved in a very sprightly, not to say mischievous, manner. After this, she gave them the three Character Dances – Scottish, Welsh and Irish – out of the same ballet. Then, while she changed her dress, the passengers took over themselves and had an eightsome reel. Jaimie and Sheena were first couple, and they danced so wonderfully that the rest of the set had a hard job to concentrate on their own dancing, so thrilled were they in watching the romantic young Scotsman, Jaimie Gordon of the famous film, *Pride o' the North*, and his beautiful red-haired partner.

Annette's next dance was the Broom Dance from *Cinderella*. Angus had made the broom for her with hazel twigs fastened to a lightweight bamboo handle – three garden canes wired together. To end the performance, there was a request – *La Sylphide* from the film *Pride o' the North*. By eleven o'clock it was all over.

'How lovely it's been!' cried Annette as they chugged back to the little jetty at Broadford. 'And oh, how beautiful the ship looks, reflected in the water! The darling *Flora MacDonald*! I shall never forget her and her nice passengers.'

14 THE EXCITING NEWS

When they got back to Airdrochan Castle there was a message from Paddy waiting for Annette: *Company off to New York. Return immediately.*

Oh, the breath-taking excitement! Annette did déboulés all round the old stone hall, finishing up with a pirouette so brilliant that she amazed herself! New York – then she was going to see it after all, and she would see it, moreover, not as a film star, but in her rightful state as a dancer, an important member of the Cosmopolitan Ballet. She sobered down a little when she remembered the cold facts. Monsieur Georges was no longer there and Miss Marty was in charge now, and Annette herself was only a very junior member of the company – in fact, in the back row of the corps de ballet, not even a soloist! Oh, well, she was going to America anyway, and that was the main thing, wasn't it? The three of them – Jaimie, Angus and Annette herself – sat down in the ingle-nook where a log fire burned cheerfully, and coffee and sandwiches had been placed on a small table by

Morag, and discussed Annette's future. Sheena, after hearing 'New York', had promptly gone to bed. She wasn't going to hear all Annette's exciting plans!

'I must go back to London at once,' Annette told the two young men. 'I mustn't delay a moment, or it may be too late. You don't know how long they've been planning it – the whole week, I expect, while the dancers have been on holiday.'

And then Angus, who up till now had said little, dropped the bombshell.

'I'm coming with you,' he said.

'Oh, thank you very much,' Annette said gratefully. 'It's most awfully nice of you to offer, but really you needn't, Angus. I can manage quite well by myself.'

'I shall come all the same,' he declared.

'Well, perhaps as far as Kyle,' agreed Annette. 'Or would it be better to go to Mallaig, and then on to Fort William? But then that would mean taking the steamer, unless perhaps Jaimie could take me over in his motor-boat. That would be better for you too, Angus. You could come back with him from Mallaig.'

'If you will just let me get a word in,' said Angus, smiling. 'I am trying to tell you, Annette, that I am coming all the way with you. I am not coming back here at all.'

Annette sat still with her mouth open in surprise, looking so much like a dark-eyed little bird that Angus longed to kiss her, but his next words did not betray his thoughts. 'Yes, all the way to London,' he repeated.

'Oh, Angus – but you *can't*,' she expostulated. 'Not all the way to London! Why, whatever would you do in London?'

'I shall do very well,' laughed Angus, 'for it is there that my work will be.'

'Your *work*?' Annette couldn't believe her ears.

'Yes, my work. Is it so surprising that I should work, now that I am eighteen years old, and have left school?'

'Oh, no, of course not, but – '

'But *what*?'

'It's London,' said Annette. 'I just can't imagine

you in London, Angus. Jaimie was funny enough – ' luckily Jaimie had gone out of the room, so didn't hear this remark ' – but *you*, Angus! I just can't imagine it.'

'You will have to get used to it, *da d'thug m'anam gradh*,' Angus told her. 'After all, what is so surprising in the fact of a Scotsman leaving his home and going to work in a city? Most Scotsmen do. Jaimie would have done so, had he not found another solution to his problem.'

'But what sort of a job have you got, Angus? Surely not in an office?' She simply couldn't imagine Angus sitting at a desk.

'I am to work with a wholesale firm that manufactures equipment for mountaineers and explorers, and fits out expeditions,' explained Angus, 'so my knowledge of the mountains of Switzerland, and also of the Highlands, will help me quite a lot. Part of my work will be to test such equipment, so I shall not spend all my time sitting in an office! I shall also spend some of it in the Advice Bureau, telling people what they ought to wear and why – to the best of my ability,' he added modestly.

'Yes, it sounds very interesting,' admitted Annette doubtfully. She still couldn't quite dissociate Angus from his mountains. Why, he would have to wear a town suit instead of a kilt!

All that night Annette tossed and turned. She was far too excited to sleep. First of all, the wonderful news

151

about America; she simply couldn't believe she was really going there after all, even if she were going as a mere member of the corps de ballet. Then there was Angus's announcement about his job in London. How lovely to have Angus in London! She wouldn't be lonely any more – and it was a fact, Annette was often very lonely in her austere convent home. Last but not least, her mother and Mr MacCrimmon were coming home from Switzerland, and she'd be able to tell them about America!

At five o'clock in the morning she slipped out of bed and went to her window. As she stood there the snow slopes turned from cold pale blue to palest pink; then to rosy pink. Although down in the village it wasn't yet light, sunrise had come to the mountain peaks. She opened her window and leaned out over the stone windowsill, listening.

Feeling she couldn't sleep any more she left the window, dressed and went downstairs. There wasn't a sound, except the ticking of the grandfather clock standing sentinel in a corner of the stone-flagged hall. Although electricity had taken the place of lamps and candles, there was still a scent of paraffin oil about the place, coupled with an indefinite smell of ancient stone. It stabbed at Annette's heart. Her home, Dancing Peel, smelled just like that. She always noticed it when she came back to it.

She pushed open the heavy oak door which was never locked, for the simple reason that no one would want to break into Airdrochan Castle for there was nothing to steal, except the heads of the various animals ornamenting the walls of hall and gunroom and a lot of threadbare carpets and curtains.

Annette walked down the grass-grown causeway and out on to the white country road at the far end. She walked on round the head of the loch, down the road to Strathaird, her eyes raised to the fantastic, splintered pinnacle ridge of Clach Glas. In front of her was Coire Ueigneich, with its mountain stream descending in waterfalls and limpid pools, and its great black pinnacle sticking out from the rock face of Blaven. It was here a pair of golden eagles nested each year, she remembered. She had never seen a golden eagle, and had a longing to do so before she went back to London. She shaded her eyes with her hands, but no eagles were to be seen. Someone, or something, was in the corrie all the same. She could see something moving up there, and as she watched, a lonely figure emerged from the great scree-slopes that filled the top part of the corrie, and began picking its way down the side of the burn. Annette waited for a while to see who it was, for in these places there are no strangers – everyone knows everyone else. Unless, of course, it was a hiker or a climber out very early. The figure had disappeared behind a great, tumbled mass of rocks, but now it reappeared on the boggy ground below and she saw that it was Sheena.

'Hello!' cried Annette when the other had drawn near enough to hear her above the noise of the waterfall. 'You're up even earlier than me, and I thought I was early! Where have you been?'

Sheena flung back her tawny hair and nodded at the mountain behind her.

'Blaven!' exclaimed Annette. 'Not right to the top?'

'Yes,' said Sheena. 'I couldn't sleep, so I got up and climbed up there in the moonlight. I saw the sun rise from the summit. It was the most beautiful thing I have ever seen!'

'Yes, I know. It is beautiful, the sunrise over the Cuillins,' said Annette, remembering her night out on the Druim Hain Ridge.

Sheena turned and stared at her.

'You know?' Then she too remembered that Annette had spent a night out on the shores of Coruisk. But what could an English girl, a Sassenach, know or feel about Skye and its mountains? There was none of the sadness and poetry of the Gael in Annette, thought Sheena, forgetting that Annette was of French extraction.

'I wonder where the golden eagles' eyrie is?' said Annette. 'I remember Jaimie telling me last year that they nested in this corrie, but I haven't seen any sign of them.'

Sheena stood still, looking back at the corrie she had just left, with its black glistening walls and scree slopes.

'You see the Unclimbed Pinnacle of Blaven?' she said. 'Well, I'll tell you something about it, something that no one else knows. You remember last year at the Skye Gathering Ball at Portree I wore eagle's feathers in my hair in the old fashion? Well, Jaimie got them for me, out of the eagles' nest up there.' She pointed at the splintered peak. 'So it is not the Unclimbed Pinnacle any more. As for the eagles – you see that speck in the sky, over the top of the third peak of Clach Glas? Well, there is your eagle. And now there is the other one – can you see it, over the top of the central gully of Blaven?'

Together they watched the two specks breathlessly as they grew larger, and presently there was a flash of great wings as the two birds soared across the corrie, and vanished into a crack in the rocks of the pinnacle.

'They have young ones in there,' said Sheena.

'How do you know?' asked Annette.

'Because one of them had a mountain hare in its talons, of course,' answered Sheena, scornful of the other's ignorance. 'Come, it is time we returned. It is half past seven.'

'My goodness, is it?' exclaimed Annette. 'Imagine! In the excitement of seeing the eagles, I had almost forgotten that Angus and I have a train to catch from Mallaig at midday. Jaimie said that we must leave directly after breakfast.'

Sheena stared at Annette jealously. Annette, it seemed, had got both the young men on a string! One of them was to take her to the mainland in his boat; the other was going to London on purpose to be in the same town with her. Sheena was sure of it! She longed for Annette to miss her train. It would just serve her right! Why should Annette Dancy go to New York when she had to stop in this island and run a guest-house! But Sheena had learned her lesson. There had been a terrible scene with Jaimie after Annette's last visit, when Sheena had kept back a letter and nearly made Annette miss an audition.

'One more such malicious prank, Sheena Mac-Donald,' Jaimie had said, 'and any friendship that ever existed between you and me will be at an end.' She knew he meant it. So this was why she warned Annette about the time, and for no other reason.

They walked back side by side round the head of the loch, reaching the castle about an hour later.

15   ANNETTE RETURNS
   TO LONDON

Angus and Annette arrived in London the following evening. Annette jumped on to a bus and went straight to the YWCA where Paddy shared a room with two other girls. She simply couldn't wait until morning to hear about America. Angus, as might be expected, accompanied her.

'There's a room where people can entertain their friends,' Annette told him when they reached the door, 'so you can come in if you wish. It's not like the convent home where men are considered beyond the pale!'

The Common Room was on the third floor, and when they reached it they found it to be very hot and noisy. Someone was strumming on a piano, four people were having a game of table tennis, and a crowd of others playing darts. They found Paddy sitting by herself in a corner darning point-shoes.

'Oh, Paddy!' cried Annette. 'I'm back, you see. I came the very moment I got your message. I'm not too late, am I? I'd die of disappointment if I were! By the way, this is Angus MacCrimmon – my step-brother. He came with me all the way from Skye, because he's got a job in London – '

'Annette – ' began Paddy, trying without success to get a word in.

'I'm so excited!' went on Annette, flinging off her mackintosh and dropping it down on the floor beside Paddy's chair, whereupon Angus gravely picked it up again. 'You can't think how thrilled I am! It's too good to be true, America, I mean, and seeing New York and everything. That was the only thing I minded when I gave up my film – not seeing New York. And now I'm going to see it after all – '

'Annette, mavourneen,' began Paddy again. 'Whist, now! Listen to me.'

And then at last Annette noticed that Paddy wasn't looking her usual happy self. There was something odd and strained about her mouth. Angus had noticed this, be it said, from the very first moment.

'What's the matter, Paddy?' Annette said, fear clutching at her heart. '*Don't* say it's America. *Don't* say I'm too late.' Paddy shook her head. 'Then what is it? What's the matter? Isn't the company going after all? Oh, that would be too awful!'

'The company is going all right,' Paddy said soberly, 'but – but – '

'But *what*?'

'It's you,' said poor Paddy. 'They've made a rule that all the people who go must be over seventeen, and you're the only one who isn't.'

'Oh, Paddy, how awful!' cried poor Annette, the tears springing to her eyes. 'I just can't believe it! Why, I'm seventeen next month. They wouldn't stick to this rule for just one month, would they?'

'I'm afraid they would,' said Paddy with a sigh. 'We've all tried our best to persuade old Marty to relent, but she's adamant. It's my guess she's made up that rule on the spot just to pay you out about those kittens. She's got her knife into you properly – we all know it. Maybe it's also because you were always Monsieur Georges's favourite. Anyway, that's why you haven't got anywhere this last season. It's not that you can't dance, Annette. We all know that you're better than anyone. Monsieur Georges knew it too.'

'Oh, darling Monsieur Georges!' cried Annette in agony. 'He would never have done such a cruel, cruel thing to me!'

'Well, there it is,' said Paddy. 'That's the way of it in the ballet. You rise or fall because someone likes or dislikes you. Everyone knows it! It's not all sheer merit. There's a bit of opportunity in it too – and a bit of luck as well.'

'I know, I know! And I always thought I had it,' said Annette through her tears. 'I always said I had dancer's luck.'

'Perhaps you still have,' put in Angus, who so far had said nothing. 'Your life isn't finished yet, Annette. You're not seventeen – '

He was unlucky in choosing just those words. It was like rubbing salt into the wound! Not seventeen, indeed! That was the cause of all her misery. She turned upon him like a fury.

'Angus! How can you say that! My life is finished! As far as ballet is concerned, I might as well be dead!'

Poor Angus didn't know what to say. He never grew used to Annette's French way of showing her feelings. If he had a grief he kept it to himself, presenting a stoic front to the world. Not so Annette – she stood in the crowded room, the tears streaming down her face, apparently not even seeing that the

people around her had stopped their games and were staring at her.

'Well, what am I to do?' she said at length. 'I suppose I'm to do something while you're all in America?'

'Yes,' said Paddy nervously. What she was going to say wasn't going to please Annette. She knew that only too well. But Annette had to know some time, so she might as well say the words, and get it over first as last.

'You're to go into pantomime,' she said. 'In the ballet, I mean, of course.'

There was a horrified silence. Then the storm broke.

'*Pantomime!*' cried Annette. 'I won't do it!'

'I'm afraid it's in your contract,' said Paddy. 'It says you can be "lent out" at the company's discretion. It wouldn't do for you to break your contract. That's never wise.'

'But *pantomime!* Oh, Paddy! What am I to be? The principal dancer?' It was obvious what Annette thought even of the principal dancer in pantomime!

'No, mavourneen, you're to understudy the principal dancer.'

When Annette had really taken this in her tears began to fall faster than ever. She turned and ran from the room, leaving Angus and Paddy staring after her, together with all the members of the YWCA, who were consumed with curiosity.

Paddy shrugged her shoulders.

161

'Och, she'll get over it, Mr – Mr – '

'MacCrimmon is my name,' said Angus, 'but I would rather you called me just Angus.'

'Well, Angus, I expect you are knowing our Annette by now! It's a temper she's got and no mistake, though I must say, being Irish meself, I'd be in a temper too if I was in her place, so I would!'

Angus, looking at Irish Paddy, with the glint of red in her hair, could well believe that!

16   THE STRANGER

Next morning she was up early. Even if she was only going to understudy the principal dancer in *Puss in Boots* in the pantomime, she must still practise. She'd been on holiday for a whole fortnight, so she'd be badly out of training. She arrived at the Cosmopolitan Theatre before ten o'clock. She supposed that the company would be rehearsing for their coming American tour in the roof studio, since the company of Czechoslovakian dancers, who had taken over the theatre for a month, would be doing their rehearsing on the stage. So she must get her own practising over before Paddy and the rest arrived. She didn't feel like meeting them just now – they'd all be talking about America and the wonderful things they were going to see and do when they got there.

She changed into practice dress and did an hour's hard barre work. She was just about to begin her centre practice when she saw that someone was standing at the door, looking in through the glass panels.

'Oh, are you looking for somebody?' she cried,

running to the door and opening it. With the joy of dancing she had forgotten her sorrows for the moment. 'I'm afraid no one's here yet. Can I help you?'

The stranger came into the studio. He had a slim, graceful figure and a finely drawn face with high cheekbones. His mouth was thin and sensitive, and he had very dark eyes, as sad as Annette's own. She noticed that he had very beautiful and expressive hands. Having expressive hands herself, Annette always noticed other people's.

'Yes, I think it is very probable that you might be able to help me,' said the strange man. Although he had a foreign air about him, his voice was English. At least, not quite English. It had a soft lilting quality that reminded Annette of somebody. Why, yes – he spoke just like Paddy!

'You're Irish?' she said.

The stranger bowed.

'I was indeed born in Ireland,' he answered. 'How clever of you to guess!'

'It was easy,' declared Annette. 'You see, you speak just like my best friend Paddy and, as Paddy says, if you've been born under the shamrock you can't hide the fact – your voice will always give you away! It's a lovely accent,' she added with a sigh of pleasure. 'I like it nearly as well as Highland Scots.'

'I am honoured,' said the stranger with a faint smile. 'But now to business. I was looking for someone of the name of Dancy – Annette Dancy.'

'Why, that's me!' cried Annette in surprise.

'I thought it might be,' said the stranger. 'When I looked in through the glass, I thought the description fitted.'

'What description?' asked Annette, mystified.

'The description given me by a very old and dear friend of mine – and of yours too,' said the stranger. 'Georges Reinholt Dutoit. Just before he died he asked to see me – I think he knew it was for the last time. "Louis, *mon cher*," he said in a whisper. "I have a little dancer for you – for your new ballet, I mean." And then he described you.'

At the mention of Monsieur Georges's name, Annette broke down.

'Oh, Mr Louis – I'm afraid I don't know your other name – I'm so terribly, terribly miserable. Since my darling Monsieur Georges's death, I don't feel I'm getting anywhere. As I said to Angus – he's my step-brother, you know – well, as I told him, I always seem to be in the wings, if you see what I mean. I'm always watching other people dance the principal roles, though I know quite well I could dance them myself, if only I got the chance. Then there's this American tour . . .' The tears began to roll down her face at the thought of it.

'It's about this American tour that I came to talk to you,' said the stranger, lighting a cigarette and stepping out of the French windows on to the flat roof. 'Come out here and we will talk. It's a view in a million! Look at all the church steeples – why, there must be a dozen or more!'

But Annette wasn't interested in church steeples; she was thinking about her career.

'You were saying, Mr Louis?'

'Oh, yes.' He dragged his eyes away from the view. 'I gather from various sources that you are not going?'

'No, I'm not. Isn't it awful?' The tears came faster. The stranger didn't seem a bit taken aback at this – he was evidently used to temperamental ballet dancers!

'That depends upon how you look at it,' he said, knocking the ash off the end of his cigarette on the edge of the parapet.

'What do you mean?'

'I mean it depends upon whether you would rather go on this American tour in the Cosmopolitan Ballet Company, or accept what I have to offer you at the Festival Hall.'

Annette's head began to spin. She clutched the edge of the parapet to steady herself.

'The Festival Hall?' she repeated. 'Then – then you are – why, you must be Louis Moreau!'

'I am,' said the stranger, smiling.

'Oh, Mr Moreau,' cried Annette, 'do please *say* something. Don't keep me guessing. I know you've got something interesting you want me to do, and I'll do anything – *anything* – rather than understudy the principal dancer in *Puss in Boots*.'

Louis Moreau's sad dark eyes lit up suddenly and danced with laughter.

'Dear me! Is that all our friend Marion Marty can find for you to do? Well, we must see if we can't go a little better! When Georges Reinholt Dutoit died, he had just finished the choreography of a play for children – a musical version of *Peter Pan*, which is to be produced in the Festival Hall at Christmas in conjunction with the Festival Ballet.'

'Oh, how lovely!' said Annette. '*Peter Pan*! I've always loved it! And do you think I might have a part in it – even a small part would be better than *Puss in Boots*,' she added humbly.

'You know,' said Mr Moreau, 'Georges Reinholt told me something that nobody else knows. He told me he choreographed this ballet with you in mind.'

'Oh, I can't believe it!' cried Annette. 'It's too wonderful! I shan't mind not going to America now – if only I can have a part in it – even a tiny little part.'

'But wouldn't you like to dance the principal role?' said Louis Moreau quickly. 'Georges Reinholt asked me to ask you, and for myself, having watched you for a whole half an hour through the door, I think we could find no one better.'

For a moment Annette was silent. She just couldn't believe her ears. It was as if Monsieur Georges had come back from the dead to help her!

'There's nothing, *nothing* I should like so much,' she said gravely. 'But what about Miss Marty? I'm bound by contract – '

'To understudy the principal dancer in *Puss in Boots*!' laughed Louis Moreau. 'Well! Well! We shall have to see about that. I do not think Marion Marty will raise any objections. If you accept my offer, I shall see about the necessary adjustment to your contract. Rehearsals begin tomorrow.'

And then he was gone as suddenly as he had come, and she was alone on the flat roof – alone with the vision of all the principal roles that had suddenly come so much nearer. One day she would be Giselle, and the Princess Aurora. She knew it!

17   THE CELEBRATION

And now you will see why this book began with the story of a mother cat and her kittens. They had a lot to do with after events. If it hadn't been for them, thought Annette, she wouldn't have antagonised Miss Marty, and she'd have been going to America with the ballet. And now she had secured the principal role in the musical version of *Peter Pan*, which would run in London for months, and it was really all due to them! She never thought that perhaps her own sensitive nature, that wouldn't allow her to turn her back on three defenceless kittens and leave them to their fate, had a little to do with it as well. It was because Annette had a nature like this that her dancing was so good. A dancer must feel deeply the emotions of joy and sorrow before she can portray these emotions in her dancing.

Annette rushed back to the convent home for lunch, her feet scarcely touching the ground. She ran up the four flights of stairs, never even stopping on the third landing to get her breath, as was her wont.

Then, after washing her hands and fondling the convent kitten for a moment she ran all the way down again to eat a huge meal. She hadn't eaten any breakfast, you see – she'd been too miserable! When she had finished her lunch she couldn't have told you a single thing she had eaten, she was so excited.

After lunch she went back to her room overlooking the rooftops. When Sister Marie Theresa came in, Annette told her about the wonderful thing that had happened.

'And so I'm going to dance in Mr Moreau's ballet, *Peter Pan*, at the Festival Hall,' she said. 'And to think that I might have been going to America and missed it!'

Sister Marie Theresa, who had heard Annette declare only that morning that her life was over because she was not going to America, smiled, not for the first time, at Annette's vagaries!

After Sister Marie Theresa had gone downstairs, summoned by an urgent bell calling her to prayer and meditation, Annette sat down on her bed and thought about Monsieur Georges and what he had done for her. It was as if he had reached out a hand from the dead and pulled her out of a rough sea on to a safe rock!

I *must* be worthy of him, she thought. I must dance as I've never danced before. My most important role; except of course the Cecchetti Casket, and that was only a school affair, and the film, *Pride o' the North*, and one can't count films.

She went to her bookcase, which was only really a couple of bookends on the top of her chest of drawers, and pulled out a battered copy of *Peter Pan*, thinking I must read the story again, although I've read it dozens of times before.

And so, sitting on the window seat of her little room, high among the chimney tops, Annette dreamed herself into the role of the immortal Peter, just as she had dreamed herself into the role of the Matchgirl, and the Little Mermaid who had no tongue, and as she would dream herself into all her principal roles, whether bewitched swan-maiden,

peasant girl, woodland spirit or a more dramatic modern heroine. She had that precious gift of imagination, without which no dancer or artist of any kind can really succeed, no matter how brilliant his or her work may be.

After tea she dressed for the celebration in her best dress, with more care than she usually took over her appearance, for she felt it was a great occasion.

'Though, as a matter of fact,' she said aloud to her reflection in the little clouded mirror in her room, 'I don't expect any of them will care in the least what I look like. I don't think Mr MacCrimmon is an authority on dress, and Mummy is much too used to me to notice what I'm wearing, or Angus either. He likes me just as well in my oldest clothes.' In the last particular she was right – Angus thought she looked beautiful in anything!

They were to meet at the Ruttlidge Hotel, which was where Jaimie and Angus had stayed for the première of *Pride o' the North*. Before Annette was inside the swing door she saw Mr and Mrs MacCrimmon. Her mother had never looked like this, she thought – so young, and happy, and suntanned! She looks younger than me! thought Annette. Younger than I *feel*, anyway. These last two days have definitely aged me. I shouldn't be surprised to find I have a grey hair!

And then she was in her mother's arms, and in Mr MacCrimmon's too, and they were all talking at once.

Angus, silent as usual, stood a little apart and listened. He wondered privately whether Mrs Dancy learned anything at all from her daughter's excited conversation about America, and Skye, and the role of the principal dancer in *Peter Pan*, or if she imagined *Peter Pan* was some sort of musical in America!

'And so you see, I've come out of the wings,' Annette said, as they walked into the dining-room.

'Yes, darling,' said Mrs Dancy, wondering what on earth her daughter meant by that.

'Yes, I'm not watching someone else dance any more,' explained Annette. 'I'm dancing the principal role myself.'

Angus, sitting opposite her, had his own ideas. She might no longer be in the wings as regards her dancing career, but she was still in the wings of life. She was only a child still. One day when she really grew up he would ask her to marry him, but it would be a long time yet.

The hotel had seven storeys, and above them an odd little tower that was reached by a narrow spiral staircase. When you reached the top you found a little circular room, furnished as a lounge. From the wide windows you got a wonderful bird's-eye view of London. Jaimie and Angus had found the place when they had stayed there before, so, after dinner Angus took Annette up there to see the lights of London.

'Oh, isn't it beautiful!' she exclaimed as they picked out the various landmarks. 'There's Piccadilly Circus,

and the Embankment, and oh, look at the bridges! They're like strings of diamonds!' She rushed from one window to another like a bit of quicksilver, Angus following more soberly. Finally she flung herself down on one of the broad window seats. 'Oh, I'm so tired! What a day I've had. Isn't everything wonderful? I'm getting used to Mummy too – I mean about her being married to your father. I expect I'm growing up . . . What's that you're humming, Angus?'

'"My love she's but a lassie yet",' said Angus. 'It's an old Scottish song written by Robbie Burns.'

'Oh, I didn't know you'd got a lassie,' said Annette. She wasn't quite sure she liked the idea of Angus having a lassie. 'Do tell me about her. Is she pretty?'

'No,' said Angus. 'She is not pretty exactly. She is sometimes very plain, but sometimes quite beautiful. At the present moment, she is not grown up.'

'Oh, you mean she's still at school? I'm surprised at you, Angus, to go and fall in love with a schoolkid!'

'She is not at school; nor is she a child,' said Angus. 'She is what you might call a betwixt and between – neither a child nor yet a woman.'

'Well, I think you might at least tell me her name,' said Annette, piqued.

'Her name is – I will tell you that another time,' said Angus. Then he added, '*Am pòs thu mi*, Annette, *mo caileag dubh?*'

'Oh, you're talking Gaelic again!' she exclaimed. 'What were you saying this time?'

'That also I will tell you another time,' said Angus, and taking her by the hand he raced down with her to the lounge where her mother and his father were waiting for them.